פרקי אבות

ArtScroll Youth Series

Rabbi Nosson Scherman
Rabbi Meir Zlotowitz
General Editors

A PROJECT OF THE

Mesorah Heritage Foundation

Published by

Mesorah Publications, ltd

ARTSCROLL

youth pirkei avos

New simplified translation and commentary by
Rabbi Avie Gold

Drawings by
Andras Halasz

Airbrush illustration by
Michael Horen

Designed by
Rabbi Sheah Brander

This Pirkei Avos is dedicated
to the memory of

Rabbi Meir Levi ז״ל
כ״ד חשון תשכ״ט

Rebbetzin Shoshana Levi ע״ה
י״ג כסלו תשל״ט

*Pioneers and molders of girls' chinuch in America,
they founded, led, taught — and set sterling personal examples —
in the Bais Yaakov of Brownsville, East New York, and Crown Heights.*

*By creating Camp Hedvah, they showed
how much an intelligently crafted summer can enrich a girl's life.*

*Their tradition lives on in Bais Yaakov d'Rav Meir and Camp Hedvah
where their legacy of* והעמידו תלמידים הרבה *continues to thrive in their children.*

תנצב״ה

RTSCROLL YOUTH SERIES®

"YOUTH PIRKEI AVOS"

Volume I: © *Copyright 1989* / Volume II: © *Copyright 1990*
One-Volume Edition © *Copyright 1995, 1998*
by Mesorah Publications, Ltd.
One-Volume Edition – First impression: February, 1995
  Second impression: March, 1998

Published by **MESORAH PUBLICATIONS, LTD.**
4401 Second Avenue / Brooklyn, N.Y 11232 / (718) 921-9000 / Fax: (718) 680-1875 / e-mail: artscroll@mesorah.com

Distributed in Israel by SIFRIATI / A. GITLER
10 Hashomrim Street / Bnei Brak 51361

Distributed in Europe by J. LEHMANN HEBREW BOOKSELLERS
20 Cambridge Terrace / Gateshead, Tyne and Wear / England NE8 1RP

Distributed in Australia and New Zealand by GOLD'S BOOK & GIFT SHOP
36 William Street / Balaclava 3183, Vic., Australia

Distributed in South Africa by KOLLEL BOOKSHOP
Shop 8A Norwood Hypermarket/ Norwood 2196 / Johannesburg, South Africa

Printed in Canada by
American Print Solutions
Custom bound by Sefercraft, Inc. / 4401 Second Avenue / Brooklyn N.Y. 11232

ISBN: 0-89906-621-6 (hard cover) / 0-89906-622-4 (paperback)

PIRKEI AVOS

Pirkei Avos teaches us how we should act toward other people and toward Hashem. These lessons may be called "good conduct" or "proper behavior." Sometimes they are called "ethics."

But who knows which conduct is good and which is bad? Who can tell us which behavior is proper and which is not? The answer is: Hashem knows; Hashem can teach us. And He did teach us when He gave us the Torah.

The Torah teaches us many mitzvos about how to treat other people and how to serve Hashem. And the Torah also tells us many stories about such great men as Avraham, Yitzchak and Yaakov who are called the אָבוֹת, Fathers, of the Jewish people, and such great women as Sarah, Rivkah, Rachel and Leah who are called our אִמָּהוֹת, Mothers. These stories tell us how these tzaddikim behaved toward others. For example, we read about Abraham and Sarah and the wonderful חֶסֶד, kindness, they showed to everyone they met, even strangers.

Many of the lessons that we learn about Jewish "ethics" can be found in these stories. That is why we call these lessons Pirkei Avos, which means the "Chapters of the Fathers." In other words, Pirkei Avos teaches the lessons of proper behavior that we learn from the stories of our Avos.

ᴥᵹ Avos — the Doorway to Torah and Life

by Rabbi Nosson Scherman

When the cold winter days are gone and the sun is setting later, it is time to get ready to learn *Pirkei Avos* every *Shabbos* afternoon. From *Pesach* until *Rosh Hashanah*, in our homes, synagogues, and study halls, we open our hearts to *Pirkei Avos*. This slim volume of the *Mishnah* is filled with rules of wise conduct and proper behavior, with short and sharp lessons that guide us in everyday life.

How is *Pirkei Avos* different from other collections of ethical sayings by wise men?

Someone once asked Rabbi Yitchok Ze'ev Soloveitchick, the famous Brisker *Rav*, "Our Sages always speak about the importance of good character and proper behavior towards our fellow human beings. They teach that losing one's temper is like worshiping idols; that shaming another person is like killing him; and that God does not like people who brag or think they are better than others. The list of such teachings is endless. But if they are truly so important, why are the requirements of good character and conduct not listed among the 613 *mitzvos* of the Torah?"

The Brisker *Rav* answered, "The Torah was given to people, not animals. A person cannot fulfill the *mitzvos* of the Torah unless he conquers and controls the animal in himself."

This idea is as old as the Torah itself. If someone truly wishes to serve God, he must rid himself of selfishness and self-interest.

Let us imagine that two different people are studying the following passage of the Talmud: "One who wishes to be pious and of extra fine character should fulfill the teachings of *Nezikin*, the section of the Talmud that deals with laws of damages and property" (*Bava Kamma* 30a).

Even a bad person would want to study these laws very carefully. Such a person cares only about himself, and he will want to know the law so that he will know how to protect himself. Such people want to know how *not* to pay for what they do wrong, how to write contracts in words that will make them a lot of profit, even if they

make someone else lose money. On the other hand, a good person will study *Nezikin*, too — but for the opposite reason. He wants to improve himself. He wants to learn how to avoid causing injury to other people and their property. He will not keep a penny to which another human being has a just claim. Obviously, when the Talmud says that good character depends on studying these laws, it is speaking to "people, not animals." A bad person can use his learning to hurt other people. A good person will study the difficult laws of *Nezikin* to discover God's rules of fair dealing and property rights, not to find ways to twist the Torah into a web that traps innocent victims.

The same passage of the Talmud continues, "One who wishes to be pious and of extra fine character should study *Avos*." By building his character on the teachings of *Avos*, one lifts himself out of the jungle where personal survival and success are the only things that count.

A person who has studied the lessons of *Avos* will have different goals than a person who is selfish, who says "I come first," and who cares only about getting what he wants. Clearly, there is a spiritual greatness in people who live according to such lessons of *Avos* as Hillel's: "Do not judge another person until you are in his place" (2:5); or Rabban Yochanan ben Zakkai's: "Even if you have studied much Torah, do not be boastful, for that is what you were created to do" (2:9).

Let no one think, however, that the lessons of *Avos* are merely the wise teachings of good people. Many good people write books about self-improvement — and they usually disagree with each other. But, *Pirkei Avos* is not just a book, it is a part of the Torah!

In Jewish tradition, a great teacher must combine high degrees of Torah knowledge, piety, and devotion to his fellow men. Their attitudes and thoughts come from their study of Torah and their service of God. That is why the ideas and teachings of such people are true even when they discuss topics that are not related to their studies or when they offer no proof for their ideas.

The teachings of *Avos* are the accumulated wisdom of such people. They are the ones that God had in mind when He said, "Let us make man in Our image after Our likeness" (*Bereishis* 1:26). This is why, for the nation of Torah, the sayings of a Hillel, and Rabban Yochanan ben Zakkai and the other Sages in *Avos* are as true as God's Own word.

Only the experts in any field can set forth the rules for success in their field. We do not ask accountants to train artists or plumbers to teach cooking. So, too, only the great Torah figures could draw the road map to be followed when searching for human perfection. That is why *Avos* is so different from collections of ethical sayings by the wise men of other nations, and from other books on self-improvement. All of the teachings in *Avos* have their roots in the Torah itself.

And that is why *Avos* begins with the words, "Moshe received the Torah from [Hashem at] Mount Sinai."

Many people study or recite *Pirkei Avos* every *Shabbos* afternoon during the summer. They study one chapter each week between *Pesach* and *Rosh Hashanah*. In this way *Pirkei Avos* is reviewed four times each year. The weekly chapter is introduced with the following *mishnah* which is taken from *Sanhedrin* 10:1.

 All Jews have a share in the World to Come. In the words of the *Navi (Yishayahu* 60:21), "Your people are all righteous *tzaddikim*; they shall inherit the land forever. They are the branch of My planting, they are the work of My hands, in which to take pride."

כָּל יִשְׂרָאֵל יֵשׁ לָהֶם חֵלֶק לָעוֹלָם הַבָּא, שֶׁנֶּאֱמַר: "וְעַמֵּךְ כֻּלָּם צַדִּיקִים, לְעוֹלָם יִירְשׁוּ אָרֶץ, נֵצֶר מַטָּעַי, מַעֲשֵׂה יָדַי לְהִתְפָּאֵר."

The weekly chapter is followed by the following *mishnah* which is taken from *Makkos* 3:18.

 Rabbi Chanania ben Akashia taught: *Hashem*, the Holy One, Blessed is He, wished to reward the Jewish people. That is why He gave them such a large Torah and so many *mitzvos*. This is what the *Navi (Yishayahu* 42:21) taught, "*Hashem* desired that the Jews should be righteous *tzaddikim*, therefore he enlarged and strengthened the Torah.

רַבִּי חֲנַנְיָא בֶּן עֲקַשְׁיָא אוֹמֵר: רָצָה הַקָּדוֹשׁ בָּרוּךְ הוּא לְזַכּוֹת אֶת יִשְׂרָאֵל, לְפִיכָךְ הִרְבָּה לָהֶם תּוֹרָה וּמִצְוֹת, שֶׁנֶּאֱמַר: "ה' חָפֵץ לְמַעַן צִדְקוֹ, יַגְדִּיל תּוֹרָה וְיַאְדִּיר."

1. **M**oshe received the Torah from Hashem at Mount Sinai. Moshe taught the Torah to Yehoshua and trained him to be the next leader of the Jews. Yehoshua taught it to the Elders who became the leaders after him. The Elders taught the Torah to the Prophets. The Prophets taught the Torah to the group of Sages known as the *Anshei Knesses Hagedolah*.

The *Anshei Knesses Hagedolah* taught three important lessons: (a) Think very carefully before judging. (b) Teach as many students as possible. (c) Make a fence to protect the Torah.

[א] **מֹשֶׁה** קִבֵּל תּוֹרָה מִסִּינַי. וּמְסָרָהּ לִיהוֹשֻׁעַ. וִיהוֹשֻׁעַ לִזְקֵנִים. וּזְקֵנִים לִנְבִיאִים. וּנְבִיאִים מְסָרוּהָ לְאַנְשֵׁי כְנֶסֶת הַגְּדוֹלָה.

הֵם אָמְרוּ שְׁלֹשָׁה דְבָרִים: הֱווּ מְתוּנִים בַּדִּין. וְהַעֲמִידוּ תַלְמִידִים הַרְבֵּה. וַעֲשׂוּ סְיָג לַתּוֹרָה.

---

1. מֹשֶׁה קִבֵּל תּוֹרָה מִסִּינַי — Moshe received the Torah from Hashem at Mount Sinai.

Some people are arrogant, others are humble. Arrogant people think they are the smartest in the world. They expect everybody to do things their way. They boast and brag about how great they are. And, of course, they never apologize for their mistakes. *Hashem* does not like arrogant people.

The opposite of arrogant is humble. People who are humble never boast or brag. They are very careful not to hurt others or make them feel bad. They seek advice and are thankful for it. *Hashem* loves humble people. Moshe was the most humble man who ever lived. That is why *Hashem* chose Moshe to receive the Torah for the Jews.

The *Gemara* (*Megillah* 29a; *Sotah* 5a) learns this lesson from the mountains around *Eretz Yisrael*. *Hashem* chose to give the Torah on Mount Sinai. Then two very tall mountains, Tavor and Carmel, came to complain. "We are taller and more beautiful than Mount Sinai," they said arrogantly. "*Hashem* should give the Torah on us!"

But *Hashem* does not like arrogance. That is why he chose Mount Sinai, a "humble" mountain.

Moshe understood this lesson and he became even more humble. That is why *Pirkei Avos* begins: מֹשֶׁה קִבֵּל תּוֹרָה מִסִּינַי, *Moshe received the Torah from Sinai*. He learned from Mount Sinai that only a humble person is worthy of receiving the Torah.

וּמְסָרָהּ לִיהוֹשֻׁעַ — Moshe taught the Torah to Yehoshua.

To learn proper behavior we must have expert teachers. The lessons of *Pirkei Avos* were taught by experts. Even more, these teachers followed their own lessons. They were wonderful examples of how good people behave. These teachers were called *Tannaim* and each one was called a *Tanna*. Each of their lessons is called a *mishnah*.

The *Tannaim* learned how to behave from their teachers. And their teachers had learned from their teachers, all the way back to the greatest teacher, Moshe *Rabbeinu*, who learned from *Hashem* Himself.

When Moshe grew old, he asked *Hashem* who the next leader of the Jews would be. *Hashem* said that it would be Yehoshua.

Yehoshua was perfect for this job. He was Moshe's best student. He went wherever Moshe went. He listened to

every word Moshe spoke. He watched everything Moshe did. And so he became a great leader like Moshe. We learn about his leadership in *Sefer Yehoshua*, the Book of Joshua.

וִיהוֹשֻׁעַ לִזְקֵנִים — Yehoshua taught it to the Elders.

After Yehoshua died, a group of wise men became the leaders of the nation. They were called "Zekeinim" or "Elders". They ruled for almost three hundred years. We do not know most of their names, but we do know some. We have all heard stories about Pinchas the grandson of Aharon, Boaz who married Rus, Elkanah father of Shmuel, Shimshon with his great strength, and the prophetess Devorah. We read about them in *Sefer Shoftim*, the Book of Judges.

לִנְבִיאִים — To the Prophets.

The period of the *Neviim*, or Prophets, began with Eli the *Kohein* and his student Shmuel. It ended about six hundred years later, soon after the Second *Beis Hamikdash* was built. Among the *Neviim* were Eliyahu, Elisha, Yishayahu, Yirmiyahu, Yechezkel, Yonah, Mordechai and Esther. Most of Tanach tells us about the *Neviim* and their teachings.

לְאַנְשֵׁי כְנֶסֶת הַגְּדוֹלָה — To the group of Sages known as the *Anshei Knesses Hagedolah*.

In the early years of the Second *Beis Hamikdash*, the leader of the Jews in *Eretz Yisrael* was Ezra *Hakohein*. He was also called Ezra *Hasofer*, the Scribe, because he wrote Torah scrolls.

Ezra had a *beis din*, or court, to help him rule. The members of Ezra's *beis din* were known as the *Anshei Knesses Hagedolah* or "the Men of the Great Assembly." This group had one hundred and twenty members, some of whom were *Neviim*. Among the more famous ones were: Daniel and his companions — Chananiah, Mishael and Azariah; Mordechai of the Purim story; Chaggai, Zechariah and Malachi, the last of the prophets; and Shimon *Hatzaddik* whom we will meet in the next *mishnah*.

הֵם אָמְרוּ שְׁלֹשָׁה דְּבָרִים — They taught three important lessons.

Certainly, the *Anshei Knesses Hagedolah* taught more than just three lessons. But these three are important for the future of Torah:

If a judge in *beis din* does not "think very carefully before

Moshe received the Torah . . . at Mount Sinai.

judging," then he may not judge correctly. People will think that the Torah is to blame for his wrong judgment.

If the community does not set up many Torah schools to "teach as many students as possible," then many people will grow up without knowing any Torah.

If the Torah leaders don't "make a fence to protect the Torah," then ignorant people will sin without realizing what they are doing.

That is why these three lessons are so very important.

וַעֲשׂוּ סְיָג לַתּוֹרָה — And make a fence to protect the Torah.
Some *mitzvos* tell us what we must do. Others tell us what we must not do. Sometimes we may make a mistake and do the wrong thing or forget to do the right thing.

The wise Torah Sages made many rules that help us remember the *mitzvos* and stop us from making mistakes. For example, the Torah tells us not to write on *Shabbos*. So the Sages made the rule that we must not even pick up a pencil on *Shabbos*. If we do hold pencils in our hands, we might forget and write.

This kind of rule is called a סְיָג, *fence*. Just as a fence stops us from entering a place where we should not be, so do these rules stop us from doing what we should not do.

But every person is different. And so every person may make a different kind of mistake. Therefore, every person should make his own "fences" that will help him to do the *mitzvos* properly.

2. After most of the older members of the *Anshei Knesses Hagedolah* grew old and passed away, Shimon *Hatzaddik* was one of the last remaining members. He taught:

The world was created so that we should do three things and without these three things the world could not exist: (a) We should study Torah. (b) We should serve *Hashem.* (c) We should act kindly to others.

[ב] שִׁמְעוֹן הַצַּדִּיק הָיָה מִשְּׁיָרֵי כְנֶסֶת הַגְּדוֹלָה. הוּא הָיָה אוֹמֵר: עַל שְׁלֹשָׁה דְבָרִים הָעוֹלָם עוֹמֵד: עַל הַתּוֹרָה. וְעַל הָעֲבוֹדָה. וְעַל גְּמִילוּת חֲסָדִים.

Serve Hashem.

Study Torah.

Act kindly.

2. שִׁמְעוֹן הַצַּדִּיק — Shimon Hatzaddik.

Shimon *Hatzaddik* was among the last and youngest of the Sages to join the *Anshei Knesses Hagedolah*. For this reason he outlived most of the others. He was the *Kohein Gadol* for forty years. During that time many miracles happened in the *Beis Hamikdash*. But when Shimon *Hatzaddik* died, the miracles stopped.

עַל שְׁלֹשָׁה דְּבָרִים הָעוֹלָם עוֹמֵד — The world was created so that we should do three things.

Each of us must act properly towards himself, towards *Hashem*, and towards other people. We must improve ourselves by learning Torah. We must serve *Hashem* through prayer and doing *mitzvos*. We must treat other people with kindness and respect.

3. Antigonus of Socho learned Torah from Shimon *Hatzaddik.* Antigonus taught:

You should not act like servants who only serve their master because they want to receive a reward. Rather, you should act like servants who serve their master because they love him and serve him without even thinking about a reward. Yet, although you love *Hashem* and wish to be close to Him, you should still fear Him so that you will not sin.

4. Yose ben Yo'ezer of Tzereidah and Yose ben Yochanan of Yerushalayim learned Torah from Shimon *Hatzaddik* and Antigonus of Socho.

Yose ben Yo'ezer of Tzereidah taught: Let your home be a meeting place for wise men; become dusty with the dust of their feet; and drink their words like a thirsty man drinks water.

5. Yose ben Yochanan of Yerushalayim taught: (a) The door of your home should be opened wide so that guests may enter easily. (b) You should treat poor people as if they were members of your family. (c) You should not chatter too much with a woman.

[ג] אַנְטִיגְנוֹס אִישׁ סוֹכוֹ קִבֵּל מִשִּׁמְעוֹן הַצַּדִּיק. הוּא הָיָה אוֹמֵר: אַל תִּהְיוּ כַּעֲבָדִים הַמְשַׁמְּשִׁין אֶת הָרַב עַל מְנָת לְקַבֵּל פְּרָס. אֶלָּא, הֱווּ כַּעֲבָדִים הַמְשַׁמְּשִׁין אֶת הָרַב שֶׁלֹּא עַל מְנָת לְקַבֵּל פְּרָס. וִיהִי מוֹרָא שָׁמַיִם עֲלֵיכֶם.

[ד] יוֹסֵי בֶּן יוֹעֶזֶר אִישׁ צְרֵדָה וְיוֹסֵי בֶּן יוֹחָנָן אִישׁ יְרוּשָׁלַיִם קִבְּלוּ מֵהֶם. יוֹסֵי בֶּן יוֹעֶזֶר אִישׁ צְרֵדָה אוֹמֵר: יְהִי בֵיתְךָ בֵּית וַעַד לַחֲכָמִים, וֶהֱוֵי מִתְאַבֵּק בַּעֲפַר רַגְלֵיהֶם, וֶהֱוֵי שׁוֹתֶה בַצָּמָא אֶת דִּבְרֵיהֶם.

[ה] יוֹסֵי בֶּן יוֹחָנָן אִישׁ יְרוּשָׁלַיִם אוֹמֵר: יְהִי בֵיתְךָ פָּתוּחַ לָרְוָחָה. וְיִהְיוּ עֲנִיִּים בְּנֵי בֵיתֶךָ. וְאַל תַּרְבֶּה שִׂיחָה עִם הָאִשָּׁה.

---

3. אַל תִּהְיוּ כַּעֲבָדִים — You should not act like servants . . .
Why do we obey instructions or follow orders from another person? There are times when we obey because of love. We love that person who gives the orders and we know that that person loves us. We love our mother and father and we show this love by obeying them.

Sometimes we follow orders because of fear. We are afraid that something bad will happen if we disobey. When the school crossing guard tells us to wait, we wait. We fear that if we didn't listen, terrible things could happen. We've all seen children wearing casts or walking with crutches after being hit by a car. May *Hashem* protect us from such things.

Often we do not really care to follow another person's orders. We have no special love for that person and we are not afraid of him. Yet we listen, because when we do we receive a reward. A worker does not have to love or fear his boss. But if he wants to get paid, he must do what the boss tells him.

We should not obey *Hashem* because we wish to receive a reward. That is not the best reason to serve *Hashem*. We should serve Him because we love Him, and we show that love by doing His *mitzvos*.

4. וֶהֱוֵי מִתְאַבֵּק בַּעֲפַר רַגְלֵיהֶם — Become dusty with the dust of their feet.
When a person walks on an unpaved road, his feet kick up the dust. If another person follows closely behind him, the second one will become covered with dust. The *Tanna* teaches that you should follow the lessons of the wise men very carefully and very closely. Then it will be as if you are walking in the dust they kicked up, and you will become full of their wisdom.

There is another explanation of this *mishnah*. In olden times the teacher would sit on a chair or a bench and the students would sit around him on the ground. Here we are taught to sit at the feet of the wise teachers so that we may learn from them.

5. וְיִהְיוּ עֲנִיִּים בְּנֵי בֵיתֶךָ — You should treat poor people as if they were members of your family.
Nobody enjoys being poor and receiving charity. When we help other people, we should be careful not to make them feel bad.

Here's an example: A boy has outgrown his *Shabbos* suit, but it is still in pretty good condition. His mother tells him to bring it to a poor family around the corner. He should not hand them the suit and say, "Here's an old suit that I don't need anymore!" That would make them feel very sad. Instead, he should say, "This suit no longer fits me, but I think it would look very good on you and you will enjoy wearing it."

וְאַל תַּרְבֶּה שִׂיחָה עִם הָאִשָּׁה — You should not chatter too much with a woman.
A husband and wife should enjoy speaking with one another. They should take pleasure in planning together to make their home "opened wide so that guests may enter easily." They should happily discuss how to "treat poor people as if they were members of the family." They should find delight in hearing each other's opinions about how to teach their children good *middos*.

Sometimes they should even make light conversation about not-so-serious matters. But this should not take up too much of their time, because a man who truly respects his wife will offer her much more than just idle chatter.

This last rule was taught even about a man's own wife, certainly it is true about another man's wife. From this the Sages learned another lesson: A man who chatters too much with women could cause bad things to happen to himself. He could leave his Torah studies, and he could end up in *Gehinnom*.

6. Yehoshua ben Perachyah and Nittai of Arbel learned Torah from Yose ben Yo'ezer and Yose ben Yochanan.

Yehoshua ben Perachyah taught: (a) Appoint a Torah teacher for yourself. (b) Gain a friend for yourself. (c) Judge all people in a good way.

7. Nittai of Arbel taught: (a) Stay far away from a bad neighbor. (b) Do not be friends with a bad person. (c) Do not think that a bad person will escape his punishment.

בְּאִשְׁתּוֹ אָמְרוּ, קַל וָחֹמֶר בְּאֵשֶׁת חֲבֵרוֹ. מִכָּאן אָמְרוּ חֲכָמִים: כָּל הַמַּרְבֶּה שִׂיחָה עִם הָאִשָּׁה — גּוֹרֵם רָעָה לְעַצְמוֹ. וּבוֹטֵל מִדִּבְרֵי תוֹרָה, וְסוֹפוֹ יוֹרֵשׁ גֵּיהִנֹּם.

[ו] יְהוֹשֻׁעַ בֶּן פְּרַחְיָה וְנִתַּאי הָאַרְבֵּלִי קִבְּלוּ מֵהֶם.

יְהוֹשֻׁעַ בֶּן פְּרַחְיָה אוֹמֵר: עֲשֵׂה לְךָ רַב. וּקְנֵה לְךָ חָבֵר. וֶהֱוֵי דָן אֶת כָּל הָאָדָם לְכַף זְכוּת.

[ז] נִתַּאי הָאַרְבֵּלִי אוֹמֵר: הַרְחֵק מִשָּׁכֵן רָע. וְאַל תִּתְחַבֵּר לָרָשָׁע. וְאַל תִּתְיָאֵשׁ מִן הַפֻּרְעָנוּת.

6. עֲשֵׂה לְךָ רַב — Appoint a Torah teacher for yourself.

It is very difficult for a person to learn Torah by himself. He can never be sure if he correctly understands what he is studying, or if his mind is playing tricks on him. But, if he learns from a teacher (who has also learned from his teacher), then he becomes part of the great chain of Torah students that stretches all the way back to Moshe *Rabbeinu*.

וּקְנֵה לְךָ חָבֵר — Gain a friend for yourself.

The word קְנֵה means "gain" but can also mean "buy". This means that a person should do whatever is necessary to win over a friend. There are many reasons why people need good friends. Here's one example.

A person may have a bad habit. He may not even realize that he has it. Most people would not bother to correct him. They would tell themselves, "It's not my business!" Or, "I don't care about that guy anyway!" But a good friend will not say these things. He will speak to his friend about this bad habit and will help him to change his ways. If a person does not have such friends, he should hire someone to be the kind of friend that will correct him when he does the wrong thing.

Another meaning of this *mishnah* is: When you study Torah, it is always better to do so with a חַבְרוּתָא, *chavrusa* or partner, than to study by yourself. That way if one of you makes a mistake, his partner will correct him. This is what Shlomo *Hamelech* meant when he wrote [*Mishlei* 4:9], "טוֹבִים הַשְּׁנַיִם מִן הָאֶחָד, Two are better than one." Our *mishnah* teaches that if you cannot find a partner to learn with, you should pay someone to be your study-partner.

וֶהֱוֵי דָן אֶת כָּל הָאָדָם לְכַף זְכוּת — Judge all people in a good way.

Here is an example. One day, Yehudis and Rivkah were waiting for the school bus. "I wonder what happened to Elisheva today!" Said Yehudis. "She's always the first one at the bus stop." When they were on the bus, Yehudis suddenly pointed out the window. "Look Rivkah, there's Elisheva! I wonder where she's going!"

Rivkah was very quick with her answer, "She must be playing hookey today. I'll bet her mother sent her to the bus on time and she walked very slowly. She missed the bus on purpose!"

"What are you saying, Rivkah?" said Yehudis. "You are speaking *lashon hara*, bad things, about Elisheva! Maybe her mother asked her to run an errand! Maybe something important happened! We must always judge people in a good way!"

You can imagine how surprised the two girls were when Elisheva came into class half an hour late. "Why are you so late this morning, Elisheva?" the teacher asked.

Elisheva answered, "Mrs. Goldstein called our house this morning. She is sick and had no milk for her children's breakfast. So Mother sent me to her house with a container of milk. That's why I missed the school bus today."

The teacher noticed Rivkah's face turn red, but she was wise enough and kind enough not to ask her about it.

7. הַרְחֵק מִשָּׁכֵן רָע וְאַל תִּתְחַבֵּר לָרָשָׁע — Stay far away from a bad neighbor; (and) do not be friends with a bad person.

If someone enters a room in which many people are smoking cigarettes, his clothing will soon smell from smoke. When he walks out of the room other people will think that he had been smoking also. But he did not smoke. The same thing happens with a person who stays in the company of bad neighbors and bad friends. Soon his *neshamah* and his reputation will become dirtied by their sins. When they are punished he may be punished along with them. Therefore we must stay far away from such people.

... if they have accepted the ruling.

8. Yehudah ben Tabbai and Shimon ben Shatach learned Torah from Yehoshua ben Perachayah and Nittai of Arbel.

Yehudah ben Tabbai taught these lessons for judges: (a) Do not act as a lawyer. (b) When the two sides stand before you, think of them both as guilty. (c) Once the two of them have left your courtroom, think of them both as innocent — if they have accepted the ruling.

[ח] יְהוּדָה בֶּן טַבַּאי וְשִׁמְעוֹן בֶּן שָׁטַח קִבְּלוּ מֵהֶם.

יְהוּדָה בֶּן טַבַּאי אוֹמֵר: אַל תַּעַשׂ עַצְמְךָ כְּעוֹרְכֵי הַדַּיָּנִין. וּכְשֶׁיִּהְיוּ בַּעֲלֵי הַדִּין עוֹמְדִים לְפָנֶיךָ, יִהְיוּ בְעֵינֶיךָ כִּרְשָׁעִים. וּכְשֶׁנִּפְטָרִים מִלְּפָנֶיךָ, יִהְיוּ בְעֵינֶיךָ כְּזַכָּאִין, כְּשֶׁקִּבְּלוּ עֲלֵיהֶם אֶת הַדִּין.

---

8. אַל תַּעַשׂ עַצְמְךָ כְּעוֹרְכֵי הַדַּיָּנִין — Do not act as a lawyer.
A lawyer helps a person prepare his case before the court. He tells his client (the person he is helping) what things to say, and what things not to say. But a judge may not do this. He must listen to what each person says, without suggesting that he say something else. A judge can decide between two people only according to their own words.

יִהְיוּ בְעֵינֶיךָ כִּרְשָׁעִים — Think of them both as guilty.
This does not mean that the judge should accuse each one of lying. It means that he should treat them both in the same

way. Even if one of them is well known for his honesty, the judge should not say to himself, ''This man never tells a lie. He must be telling the truth now also.'' Instead, the judge must think carefully about what each person says. Then he can make a fair judgment.

יִהְיוּ בְעֵינֶיךָ כְּזַכָּאִין — Think of them both as innocent.
Do not think, ''The one who lost the case is a liar. He knew he was wrong and he lied in order to win.'' Instead, say to yourself, ''He really thought he was right. He didn't lie. He made a mistake.''

9. Shimon ben Shatach also taught a lesson for judges:

Ask the witnesses a lot of questions, but be careful that your words should not teach them how to lie.

10. Shemayah and Avtalyon learned Torah from Yehudah ben Tabbai and Shimon ben Shatach.

Shemayah taught: (a) You should love work. (b) You should hate being in a position of power. (c) You should not be too friendly with government officials.

11. Avtalyon taught a lesson for teachers. He said:

O wise men, be careful with your words, for someday you may be forced to leave your city to live in a place which has "bad water." When your students follow you there, they may drink that bad water and die. This will cause a *chillul Hashem*.

[ט] שִׁמְעוֹן בֶּן שָׁטַח אוֹמֵר:
הֱוֵי מַרְבֶּה לַחֲקוֹר אֶת הָעֵדִים, וֶהֱוֵי זָהִיר בִּדְבָרֶיךָ, שֶׁמָּא מִתּוֹכָם יִלְמְדוּ לְשַׁקֵּר.

[י] שְׁמַעְיָה וְאַבְטַלְיוֹן קִבְּלוּ מֵהֶם. שְׁמַעְיָה אוֹמֵר: אֱהַב אֶת הַמְּלָאכָה. וּשְׂנָא אֶת הָרַבָּנוּת. וְאַל תִּתְוַדַּע לָרָשׁוּת.

[יא] אַבְטַלְיוֹן אוֹמֵר:
חֲכָמִים, הִזָּהֲרוּ בְדִבְרֵיכֶם, שֶׁמָּא תָחוּבוּ חוֹבַת גָּלוּת וְתִגְלוּ לִמְקוֹם מַיִם הָרָעִים. וְיִשְׁתּוּ הַתַּלְמִידִים הַבָּאִים אַחֲרֵיכֶם, וְיָמוּתוּ. וְנִמְצָא שֵׁם שָׁמַיִם מִתְחַלֵּל.

9. שֶׁמָּא מִתּוֹכָם יִלְמְדוּ לְשַׁקֵּר — Your words should not teach them how to lie.

A mother once came into the kitchen and found that someone had cut a chunk out of her freshly baked cake. "Who took cake without permission?" she called out.

"What cake?" replied Yossi from the next room.

Later that night she asked Yossi, "How did you manage to eat that big piece of cake all by yourself?"

This time Yossi replied, "I guess I did the wrong thing, Mommy. I'm sorry."

Yossi gave a different answer when his mother asked the question differently. In the same way when the judge questions the witnesses, he must be careful of the words he uses. Otherwise his questions may teach them how to lie.

10. אֱהַב אֶת הַמְּלָאכָה — You should love work.

Every person must keep himself occupied. When a person has too much free time, he begins to find ways to use that time. If he fills his day with study, work and even with some healthy play, then his time is not wasted. His mind and his body always do useful things and he accomplishes a lot. But if he wastes his time sitting around doing nothing useful, his mind will soon be filled with silly ideas. Little by little, this foolishness will become the most important part of his life. According to another *mishnah* (Kesubos 5:5), this will lead either to sin or to insanity.

וּשְׂנָא אֶת הָרַבָּנוּת — You should hate being in a position of power.

Being in a position of power is not easy. First of all, a person in a powerful position may have many jealous enemies who seek to do him harm. Secondly, a powerful person must always make important decisions. A wrong decision, even if it is only a little bit wrong, can cause great problems. For example, a general must think very carefully

before he leads his army into battle. If his plans go wrong, he and all of his soldiers may be captured or even killed.

Thirdly, a person in a position of power must always remember that *Hashem* put him into that position to set an example for others to follow. If he becomes selfish, or if he mistreats those under him, *Hashem* will judge him harshly. In fact, the *Gemara* (*Pesachim* 87b) tells us that kingship sometimes makes a person die young. That is why many of the prophets outlived four kings each. For example, the prophets Yeshayahu and Hoshea each prophesied during the reigns of Uziyahu, Yosam, Achaz, and Yechizkiyahu.

וְאַל תִּתְוַדַּע לָרָשׁוּת — You should not be too friendly with government officials.

This is explained in chapter 2, *mishnah* 3.

11. חֲכָמִים הִזָּהֲרוּ בְדִבְרֵיכֶם — O wise men, be careful with your words.

When you teach your students, you must choose your words carefully. Do not speak in a way that can be misunderstood. Your own students may be used to your way of teaching. They will study your lessons until they are sure that they understand exactly what you meant to say.

But someday you may have to travel to another place. In this new place you will find "bad water." That is, you will find students who will not study everything you say carefully. Instead, they will misinterpret whatever you teach. They will act sinfully and say, "We are only doing what is written in the Torah. This is what our teacher taught us." Others will learn from them, thinking that they are following the Torah.

The *mishnah* calls these false interpretations of the Torah "bad water." Just as bad water makes a person's body sick, these false teachings make a person's soul sick. And they are a *chillul Hashem*, a disgrace to God's Holy Name.

12. Hillel and Shammai learned Torah from Shemayah and Avtalyon.

Hillel taught:

Be one of the followers of Aaron the *Kohein Gadol.* You can do this by loving peace, running after peace, loving people and bringing them closer to the Torah.

[יב] הִלֵּל וְשַׁמַּאי קִבְּלוּ מֵהֶם. הִלֵּל אוֹמֵר: הֱוֵי מִתַּלְמִידָיו שֶׁל אַהֲרֹן. אוֹהֵב שָׁלוֹם וְרוֹדֵף שָׁלוֹם, אוֹהֵב אֶת הַבְּרִיּוֹת וּמְקָרְבָן לַתּוֹרָה.

12. הֱוֵי מִתַּלְמִידָיו שֶׁל אַהֲרֹן — **Be one of the followers of Aharon the *Kohein Gadol.***

How did Aharon run after peace? Whenever Aharon saw that two people were angry at each other, he would approach one of them and say, "Do you realize how sorry your friend is for making you angry? He really is so ashamed of himself that he is too embarrassed to ask you for forgiveness. That is why he wants me to speak to you for him. Won't you please forgive him?" Then Aharon would go to the other person and say the exact same thing. And the next time the two "enemies" met they would greet each other as old friends.

How did Aharon bring people closer to the Torah? Whenever Aharon knew that a person had sinned, he would approach that person, put his hand on that person's shoulder and talk to him in a very friendly way. Usually the sinner would think, "Look how friendly Aharon is to me. He must really think I'm someone special. If he only knew about my bad ways, he would never even speak to me again. If I want Aharon to remain my friend, I'd better start behaving myself." And he would mend his ways and follow the laws more carefully.

13. Hillel also taught: (a) A person who spreads his name will lose his name. (b) A person who does not add to his Torah knowledge will forget what he already knows. (c) A person who does not study Torah at all does not deserve to live. (d) A person who uses his Torah knowledge selfishly will lose his reward.

14. Hillel also taught that we should always ask ourselves three questions: (a) If I am not for myself, who will be for me? (b) And if I am for myself, what am I? (c) And if not now, when?

15. Shammai taught: (a) Make a regular schedule for your Torah study. (b) Say a little but do a lot. (c) Greet all people cheerfully.

16. Rabban Gamliel taught: (a) Appoint a Torah teacher for yourself so that you will be free of doubt. (b) Do not guess how much *ma'aser* to give.

[יג] הוּא הָיָה אוֹמֵר: נְגִיד שְׁמָא אֲבַד שְׁמֵהּ. וּדְלָא מוֹסִיף יָסֵף. וּדְלָא יַלִיף קְטָלָא חַיָּב. וּדְאִשְׁתַּמַּשׁ בְּתָגָא חֲלָף.

[יד] הוּא הָיָה אוֹמֵר: אִם אֵין אֲנִי לִי, מִי לִי? וּכְשֶׁאֲנִי לְעַצְמִי, מָה אֲנִי? וְאִם לֹא עַכְשָׁו, אֵימָתַי?

[טו] שַׁמַּאי אוֹמֵר: עֲשֵׂה תוֹרָתְךָ קֶבַע. אֱמֹר מְעַט וַעֲשֵׂה הַרְבֵּה. וֶהֱוֵי מְקַבֵּל אֶת כָּל הָאָדָם בְּסֵבֶר פָּנִים יָפוֹת.

[טז] רַבָּן גַּמְלִיאֵל הָיָה אוֹמֵר: עֲשֵׂה לְךָ רַב, וְהִסְתַּלֵּק מִן הַסָּפֵק. וְאַל תַּרְבֶּה לְעַשֵּׂר אֲמָדוֹת.

13. נְגִיד שְׁמָא אֲבַד שְׁמֵהּ — **A person who spreads his name will lose his name.**

People who always do good things often become famous and are honored by others. They may not seek fame or honor, but it comes to them anyway. A yeshivah may place their names on the school's wall. A hospital to which they have donated a large amount of money may put their name on an ambulance. They may be asked to speak or to be the guests of honor at a dinner. Their honor comes for only one reason, they are worthy of it. Such honor lasts forever.

Some people only do good deeds in order to become famous. They will not give any donations to a yeshivah, unless their name is placed on the building wall. They will not give any money to a hospital to buy a new ambulance, unless their name is printed on the side of the ambulance. They will not help with a charity dinner, unless they are allowed to make a speech at the dinner. Their charity is real charity. Their speech may even be very interesting. And their honor is real honor. But it comes for two reasons: First, because they seek it; second because they deserve it. Such honor may last very long, but at some time it will begin to fade.

וּדְלָא מוֹסִיף יָסֵף — **A person who does not add to his Torah knowledge will forget what he already knows.**

We must always review our Torah lessons and study new portions. In this way our Torah knowledge will grow and grow. But if someone does not do this, he will soon know less and less. In the *Gemara* (*Yerushalmi Berachos* 9:5) we are taught: "יוֹם תַּעַזְבֵנִי יוֹמַיִם אֶעֶזְבֶךָ, If you leave me (the Torah) for one day, I will leave you for two days." This is like two people who are traveling in different directions on the same road. After one day the two travelers will be two days away from each other. After two days, they will be four days apart.

וּדְאִשְׁתַּמַּשׁ בְּתָגָא חֲלָף — **A person who uses his Torah knowledge selfishly will lose his reward.**

Torah study is required of everybody. At the very least, one must study the *mitzvos* that affect his everyday life. Therefore one who has gained much Torah knowledge should not use it in a selfish way. He must share his knowledge with others. Although, everyone must show respect for a Torah scholar, the scholar may not make harsh or selfish demands on others. If he does such things, then they will be considered as part of the reward for his Torah learning. And he will not get the full reward that he should have received in *Gan Eden*.

14. אִם אֵין אֲנִי לִי — **If I am not for myself.**

This means, if I do not fulfill the *mitzvos* that *Hashem* requires of me, will anybody else do them for me? "And even if I am for myself," and I do many *mitzvos*, how much can one person accomplish all by himself? And if I do not do as much as I can while I'm still young and full of strength and vigor, when will I be able to do it?

16. עֲשֵׂה לְךָ רַב — **Appoint a Torah teacher for yourself.]**

These same words appeared earlier (*mishnah* 6). There we were taught to appoint a teacher so that we would become part of the great chain of Torah students that stretches all the way back to Moshe *Rabbeinu*. Here we are taught to choose a *rav* to whom we will bring all of our questions in *halachah*. This is why the *Tanna* adds, "וְהִסְתַּלֵּק מִן הַסָּפֵק, so that you will be free of doubt." If you will choose a *rav* who will decide all of your halachic problems, then you will always be certain of the correct way to act.

וְאַל תַּרְבֶּה לְעַשֵּׂר אֲמָדוֹת — **Do not guess how much ma'aser to give.**

Before eating from the crops that grow in *Eretz Yisrael*, *ma'aser* must be set aside. *Ma'aser* is exactly one-tenth of the harvest and is given to a *Levi*. In order to be sure that he sets aside the proper amount for *ma'aser*, a person must first measure the size of his crop. If he is too lazy to take a correct measurement and he just guesses how much to set aside, he may not set aside enough. Or he may set aside too much. In either case, he did not fulfill the *mitzvah* of *ma'aser* properly.

Make a regular schedule for your Torah study.

17. Shimon the son of Rabban Gamliel taught: (a) All my life I have been raised among the Sages and I have not found anything better than silence. (b) Merely studying Torah is not as important as doing what the Torah tells us to do. (c) Anyone who talks too much brings on sin.

18. Rabban Shimon ben Gamliel taught:

The world continues to stand because of three things: (a) Because of justice; (b) because of truth; and (c) because of peace.

We learn this from the words of the *Navi* (*Zechariah* 8:16): "Truth and justice, peace shall rule in your gates."

[יז] שִׁמְעוֹן בְּנוֹ אוֹמֵר: כָּל יָמַי גָּדַלְתִּי בֵּין הַחֲכָמִים, וְלֹא מָצָאתִי לַגּוּף טוֹב אֶלָּא שְׁתִיקָה. וְלֹא הַמִּדְרָשׁ הוּא הָעִקָּר, אֶלָּא הַמַּעֲשֶׂה. וְכָל הַמַּרְבֶּה דְבָרִים מֵבִיא חֵטְא.

[יח] רַבָּן שִׁמְעוֹן בֶּן גַּמְלִיאֵל אוֹמֵר: עַל שְׁלֹשָׁה דְבָרִים הָעוֹלָם קַיָּם — עַל הַדִּין וְעַל הָאֱמֶת וְעַל הַשָּׁלוֹם. שֶׁנֶּאֱמַר: "אֱמֶת וּמִשְׁפַּט שָׁלוֹם שִׁפְטוּ בְּשַׁעֲרֵיכֶם."

18. עַל הַדִּין וְעַל הָאֱמֶת וְעַל הַשָּׁלוֹם — **Because of justice; because of truth; and because of peace.**

The Talmud (*Yerushalmi Ta'anis* 4:2) explains that all three are really one. When people know that the courts of justice will uncover their false claims, they will be afraid to lie. In this way justice brings truth. And once there is justice and truth, all arguments will be ended and there will be peace. That is what the *Navi* Zechariah teaches us, "[When there is] truth and justice, [then] peace shall rule in your gates."

[א] **רַבִּי** אוֹמֵר: אֵיזוֹ הִיא דֶרֶךְ יְשָׁרָה שֶׁיָּבֹר לוֹ הָאָדָם? כָּל שֶׁהִיא תִפְאֶרֶת לְעֹשֶׂהָ וְתִפְאֶרֶת לוֹ מִן הָאָדָם. וֶהֱוֵי זָהִיר בְּמִצְוָה קַלָּה כְּבַחֲמוּרָה, שֶׁאֵין אַתָּה יוֹדֵעַ מַתַּן שְׂכָרָן שֶׁל מִצְוֹת. וֶהֱוֵי מְחַשֵּׁב הֶפְסֵד מִצְוָה כְּנֶגֶד שְׂכָרָהּ, וּשְׂכַר עֲבֵרָה כְּנֶגֶד הֶפְסֵדָהּ.

הִסְתַּכֵּל בִּשְׁלֹשָׁה דְבָרִים, וְאֵין אַתָּה בָא לִידֵי עֲבֵרָה. דַּע מַה לְמַעְלָה מִמְּךְ: עַיִן רוֹאָה; וְאֹזֶן שׁוֹמַעַת; וְכָל מַעֲשֶׂיךָ בַּסֵּפֶר נִכְתָּבִים.

[ב] **רַבָּן גַּמְלִיאֵל** בְּנוֹ שֶׁל רַבִּי יְהוּדָה הַנָּשִׂיא אוֹמֵר: יָפֶה תַלְמוּד תּוֹרָה עִם דֶּרֶךְ אֶרֶץ, שֶׁיְּגִיעַת שְׁנֵיהֶם מְשַׁכַּחַת עָוֹן. וְכָל תּוֹרָה שֶׁאֵין עִמָּהּ מְלָאכָה, סוֹפָהּ בְּטֵלָה וְגוֹרֶרֶת עָוֹן.

וְכָל הָעוֹסְקִים עִם הַצִּבּוּר, יִהְיוּ עוֹסְקִים עִמָּהֶם לְשֵׁם שָׁמַיִם, שֶׁזְּכוּת אֲבוֹתָם מְסַיַּעְתָּם, וְצִדְקָתָם עוֹמֶדֶת לָעַד. וְאַתֶּם, מַעֲלֶה אֲנִי עֲלֵיכֶם שָׂכָר הַרְבֵּה כְּאִלּוּ עֲשִׂיתֶם.

1. abbi [Yehudah *Hanassi*] taught:
(a) What is the proper path for a person to choose for himself? He should choose a path that is good for himself and causes other people to admire him. (b) Be just as careful in doing a *mitzvah* that you think is not important as you are in doing a *mitzvah* that you think is important, because you do not know which *mitzvah* will earn you a greater reward. (c) Compare the amount you spend doing a *mitzvah* with the reward you will receive for doing it; and compare the amount you gain by doing a sin with the punishment you will receive for doing it.

(d) Think of three things and you will not sin. Know that these three things are above you: An Eye is watching you; an Ear is listening to you; and whatever you say or do is written in a Book.

2. Rabban Gamliel the son of R' Yehudah *Hanassi* taught: (a) It is good to combine Torah study with a job, for working hard at both of them stops a person from sinning. Even more, any Torah study that is not combined with a job may end up as nothing and may even lead to sin.

(b) When you work for the community, you should work for *Hashem's* sake, then the good deeds of your fathers will help you, for their good deeds last forever. And even though you were helped by their good deeds, *Hashem* will still reward you as if you did everything by yourself.

---

1. תִּפְאֶרֶת לְעֹשֶׂהָ וְתִפְאֶרֶת לוֹ מִן הָאָדָם — **That is good for him and causes other people to like him.**

Most of the *middos* have opposites and in-betweens. For every *middah*, we must try to follow the in-between path. Let us take spending money as an example. Some people spend or give away every dollar they earn. They are called spend-thrifts. Other people do just the opposite. They save as much money as they can, almost never give charity, and buy only what they absolutely must. These people are called misers.

Everyone likes a spendthrift. He's a good customer, so the shopkeepers like him. He gives away a lot, so the poor like him. He buys his friends presents, so they like him. He eats expensive meals, so the restaurant owner likes him. But all this spending is not good for himself. Soon he will have no more money to buy the things he needs.

A miser is just the opposite. Nobody likes him. He's not a good customer; he never gives charity; he never buys presents; and he eats very, very little. Yet, in a selfish way, he is doing good for himself. Since he saves all his money, he is very likely to become rich.

In between the miser and the spendthrift is the person who spends as much as he has to, and gives as much charity as he can afford. But still he makes sure to save enough money in case of an emergency. This person acts with נְדִיבוּת, *generosity*. He follows "a path that is good for himself and causes other people to admire him."

עַיִן רוֹאָה וְאֹזֶן שׁוֹמַעַת וְכָל מַעֲשֶׂיךָ בַּסֵּפֶר נִכְתָּבִים — **An Eye is watching you; an Ear is listening to you; and whatever you say or do is written in a Book.**

Many years ago, before the invention of cameras and tape recorders, it was very difficult to understand this *mishnah*. But today we can see things happening in front of us on film, even though they really took place many years ago. And we can hear recordings of things said a long time ago.

The Eye, Ear and Book of our *mishnah* all refer to *Hashem*. He sees and hears everything, and never forgets anything. It is as if a camera and a microphone are recording whatever you do and storing your actions and words on film and tapes.

It is good to combine Torah study with a job.

2. וְכָל תּוֹרָה שֶׁאֵין עִמָּהּ מְלָאכָה סוֹפָהּ בְּטֵלָה וְגוֹרֶרֶת עָוֹן — Any Torah study that is not combined with a job may end up as nothing and may even lead to sin.

The words דֶּרֶךְ אֶרֶץ and מְלָאכָה are translated "job". But they really mean a way of earning money for himself and his family. A man must provide his family with food, clothing and a place to live. Most people have to spend a good part of their day at their jobs in order to support themselves. Some people do not have to work at a job because

they have saved up enough money to supply their needs. Others are supported by relatives or by a *Kollel*. They can spend their entire day studying Torah even if they don't have a job.

But if someone has nobody to support him and he does not support himself, his family will soon be hungry and their clothing will be ragged. He will not be able to continue his studies. And he may even turn dishonest in order to supply his family's needs.

3. (c) Be careful of government officials, for they become friends with a person only for their own good. They act friendly when it is good for them, but they do not help someone when he needs help.

[ג] הֱווּ זְהִירִין בָּרְשׁוּת, שֶׁאֵין מְקָרְבִין לוֹ לְאָדָם אֶלָּא לְצֹרֶךְ עַצְמָן. נִרְאִין כְּאוֹהֲבִין בִּשְׁעַת הֲנָאָתָן, וְאֵין עוֹמְדִין לוֹ לְאָדָם בִּשְׁעַת דָּחְקוֹ.

4. He also used to teach:

Fulfill *Hashem's mitzvos* as you fulfill own desires, then *Hashem* will fulfill your desires as if they were His own.

Destroy your own desires when they are different from *Hashem's*, then *Hashem* will destroy the desires of others when they are different from yours.

[ד] הוּא הָיָה אוֹמֵר: עֲשֵׂה רְצוֹנוֹ כִּרְצוֹנֶךָ, כְּדֵי שֶׁיַּעֲשֶׂה רְצוֹנְךָ כִּרְצוֹנוֹ.

בַּטֵּל רְצוֹנְךָ מִפְּנֵי רְצוֹנוֹ, כְּדֵי שֶׁיְּבַטֵּל רְצוֹן אֲחֵרִים מִפְּנֵי רְצוֹנֶךָ.

5. Hillel taught: (a) Do not separate yourself from the community. (b) As long as you live, do not think that you will never sin. (c) Do not judge another person until you are in his place. (d) Keep your private thoughts to yourself, even if you think nobody else is listening, because in the end what you say will be heard by others. (e) Do not say, "I will study when I have free time," for you may never have free time.

6. He used to teach: (a) A fool cannot be afraid of sin. (b) A person who has not studied Torah cannot be very careful about mitzvos. (c) A person who is too shy to ask questions cannot learn. (d) A person who gets angry easily cannot teach. (e) A person who spends too much time in business cannot become a Torah scholar. (f) In a place where there are no leaders, try to be a leader.

7. Hillel once saw a skull floating on the water. He said to the skull, "Because you drowned others, you were drowned. And those who drowned you will also be drowned."

[ה] הִלֵּל אוֹמֵר: אַל תִּפְרוֹשׁ מִן הַצִּבּוּר. וְאַל תַּאֲמִין בְּעַצְמְךָ עַד יוֹם מוֹתְךָ. וְאַל תָּדִין אֶת חֲבֵרְךָ עַד שֶׁתַּגִּיעַ לִמְקוֹמוֹ. וְאַל תֹּאמַר דָּבָר שֶׁאִי אֶפְשָׁר לִשְׁמֹעַ, שֶׁסּוֹפוֹ לְהִשָּׁמַע. וְאַל תֹּאמַר לִכְשֶׁאֶפָּנֶה אֶשְׁנֶה, שֶׁמָּא לֹא תִפָּנֶה.

[ו] הוּא הָיָה אוֹמֵר: אֵין בּוּר יְרֵא חֵטְא. וְלֹא עַם הָאָרֶץ חָסִיד. וְלֹא הַבַּיְשָׁן לָמֵד. וְלֹא הַקַּפְּדָן מְלַמֵּד. וְלֹא כָל הַמַּרְבֶּה בִסְחוֹרָה מַחְכִּים. וּבִמְקוֹם שֶׁאֵין אֲנָשִׁים הִשְׁתַּדֵּל לִהְיוֹת אִישׁ.

[ז] אַף הוּא רָאָה גֻלְגֹּלֶת אַחַת שֶׁצָּפָה עַל פְּנֵי הַמָּיִם. אָמַר לָהּ, "עַל דַּאֲטֵפְתְּ אַטְפוּךְ. וְסוֹף מְטַיְפָיִךְ יְטוּפוּן."

---

5. אַל תִּפְרוֹשׁ מִן הַצִּבּוּר — **Do not separate yourself from the community.**

When trouble strikes the community, everyone must join in the sorrow. For example, if a row of houses is destroyed by fire, the family whose home remained standing should not say, "Well, that's their problem, not ours." Instead, they should feel just as sorrowful as if their own home was burned. And they should offer as much help as possible to the unfortunate ones.

וְאַל תַּאֲמִין בְּעַצְמְךָ עַד יוֹם מוֹתְךָ — **As long as you live, do not think that you will never sin.**

Nobody can ever know for sure that his *yetzer hara* will never lead him to sin. The *Gemara* (*Berachos* 29a) tells us the story of Yochanan who was the *Kohein Gadol* (High Priest) for eighty years. Yet, at the end of his life, he became a sinner. So we see that everybody must always be on guard against his *yetzer hara*.

וְאַל תָּדִין אֶת חֲבֵרְךָ עַד שֶׁתַּגִּיעַ לִמְקוֹמוֹ — **Do not judge another person until you are in his place.**

When we see our friend doing the wrong thing, we should not call him "wicked" or "bad." Maybe if we were in the same situation we would act in an even worse way. Instead of judging our friend, we should remind him in a nice way that what he is doing is wrong.

שֶׁסּוֹפוֹ לְהִשָּׁמַע — **Because, in the end, what you say will be heard.**

Shlomo *Hamelech* (King Solomon) taught: "Even in your thoughts do not curse a king; even in your private bedroom, do not curse a wise man; for the birds in the sky will carry your voice, and the winged creatures will repeat your words" (*Koheles* 10:20).

6. וְלֹא עַם הָאָרֶץ חָסִיד — **A person who has not studied Torah cannot be very careful about mitzvos.**

Some people think that they can do all the *mitzvos* even if they don't spend any time studying the Torah. But they are wrong. If someone does not learn Torah, he will not know how to do the *mitzvos* correctly.

וְלֹא הַקַּפְּדָן מְלַמֵּד — **A person who gets angry easily cannot teach.**

If a teacher does not have patience with his students, they will be afraid to ask questions. And as the *Mishnah* just said, "A person who doesn't ask questions cannot learn."

7. עַל דַּאֲטֵפְתְּ אַטְפוּךְ וְסוֹף מְטַיְפָיִךְ יְטוּפוּן — **Because you drowned others, you were drowned; and those who drowned you will also be drowned.**

Nothing happens without a reason. *Hashem* punishes sinfulness מִדָּה כְּנֶגֶד מִדָּה, measure for measure. In other words, the punishment always fits the crime. When something bad happens, the victim should examine his deeds. Perhaps he did something wrong and is being punished. Of course his sore throat was caused by germs. But perhaps these germs would not have entered his throat, if he had not spoken *lashon hara*, bad about others.

In the same way, if a person was the victim of a crime, he should consider it as a punishment for some sin that he did. But at the same time, he should not think that his attacker will escape without punishment.

8. He used to teach that too much of certain things are not good for a person: (a) The more flesh, the more worms; (b) the more property, the more problems; (c) the more wives, the more witchcraft; (d) the more maids, the more sins; (e) the more servants, the more stealing.

But about other things he taught that the more you have the better it is: (a)The more Torah, the more life; (b) the more study, the more wisdom; (c) the more advice, the more understanding; (d) the more charity, the more peace.

If a person has gained a good name, he has gained something good for himself. If a person has gained Torah knowledge, he has gained himself life in the World to Come.

9. Rabban Yochanan ben Zakkai learned Torah from Hillel and Shammai. He taught:

Even if you have studied a lot of Torah, do not be boastful, for that is what you were created to do.

10. Rabban Yochanan ben Zakkai had five main students. They were R' Eliezer ben Hyrkanos, R' Yehoshua ben Chanania, R' Yose the *Kohein*, R' Shimon ben Nesanel and R' Elazar ben Arach.

11. He used to praise each of his students:

[ח] הוּא הָיָה אוֹמֵר: מַרְבֶּה בָשָׂר, מַרְבֶּה רִמָּה; מַרְבֶּה נְכָסִים, מַרְבֶּה דְאָגָה; מַרְבֶּה נָשִׁים, מַרְבֶּה כְשָׁפִים; מַרְבֶּה שְׁפָחוֹת, מַרְבֶּה זִמָּה; מַרְבֶּה עֲבָדִים, מַרְבֶּה גָזֵל.

מַרְבֶּה תוֹרָה, מַרְבֶּה חַיִּים; מַרְבֶּה יְשִׁיבָה, מַרְבֶּה חָכְמָה; מַרְבֶּה עֵצָה, מַרְבֶּה תְבוּנָה; מַרְבֶּה צְדָקָה, מַרְבֶּה שָׁלוֹם. קָנָה שֵׁם טוֹב, קָנָה לְעַצְמוֹ. קָנָה לוֹ דִבְרֵי תוֹרָה, קָנָה לוֹ חַיֵּי הָעוֹלָם הַבָּא.

[ט] רַבָּן יוֹחָנָן בֶּן זַכַּאי קִבֵּל מֵהִלֵּל וּמִשַּׁמַּאי. הוּא הָיָה אוֹמֵר: אִם לָמַדְתָּ תוֹרָה הַרְבֵּה, אַל תַּחֲזִיק טוֹבָה לְעַצְמְךָ, כִּי לְכָךְ נוֹצָרְתָּ.

[י] חֲמִשָּׁה תַלְמִידִים הָיוּ לוֹ לְרַבָּן יוֹחָנָן בֶּן זַכַּאי, וְאֵלּוּ הֵן: רַבִּי אֱלִיעֶזֶר בֶּן הֻרְקָנוֹס, רַבִּי יְהוֹשֻׁעַ בֶּן חֲנַנְיָא, רַבִּי יוֹסֵי הַכֹּהֵן, רַבִּי שִׁמְעוֹן בֶּן נְתַנְאֵל, וְרַבִּי אֶלְעָזָר בֶּן עֲרָךְ.

[יא] הוּא הָיָה מוֹנֶה שִׁבְחָן:

---

8. מַרְבֶּה בָשָׂר מַרְבֶּה רִמָּה **— The more flesh, the more worms.**
People who stuff themselves on heavy, fatty foods may get pleasure from their meals and may satisfy their huge appetites. But fat people are more likely to get sick than thin people. The more flesh a person has, the more chance he has of becoming sick with the "worms" of disease.

מַרְבֶּה נָשִׁים מַרְבֶּה כְשָׁפִים **— The more wives, the more witchcraft.**
In olden times, a man was allowed to marry many wives. Often the wives would be jealous of one another and this would cause a lot of trouble. In fact, when a man had more than one wife, each wife was called a צָרָה (trouble) to the others. Sometimes one wife's jealousy would cause her to try anything — even witchcraft — to become her husband's favorite wife.

מַרְבֶּה שְׁפָחוֹת מַרְבֶּה זִמָּה; מַרְבֶּה עֲבָדִים מַרְבֶּה גָזֵל **— The more maids, the more sins; the more servants, the more stealing.**
Rich people used to have slaves and maids working in their homes. These servants did not care to follow the laws of the Torah. The Sages did not think this was a good idea. Here we learn that if there are many such servants and maids in someone's house, that house will soon be full of stealing and other sins.

9. כִּי לְכָךְ נוֹצָרְתָּ **— For that is what you were created to do.**
Birds were created with wings so that they could fly. Fish were created with fins so that they could swim. Can a bird boast to a fish, "I can travel through the sky!"? Can a fish boast to a bird, "I can swim under the sea!"? Of course not. They are only doing what they were created to do.

People were created with intelligence and understanding so that they could study *Hashem's* Torah. Can a person boast, "I have learned much Torah!"? Of course not. He is only doing what he was created to do.

10. חֲמִשָּׁה תַלְמִידִים **— Five main students.**
This *mishnah* seems to teach us very little. It is just a list of the names of five people! But really we can improve ourselves very much by just mentioning the names of these *tzaddikim*. For their names remind us of them, and thinking of them reminds us of what they did and what they taught. And these lessons help us to become better people. That is why Shlomo *Hamelech* taught us, "זֵכֶר צַדִּיק לִבְרָכָה," Mentioning a *tzaddik's* name is a blessing (*Mishlei* 10:7).

11. הוּא הָיָה מוֹנֶה שִׁבְחָן **— He used to praise each of his students.**
We learned in the last *mishnah* that just mentioning a *tzaddik's* name will make us better people. Certainly when

R' Eliezer ben Hyrkanos is like a cemented pool that does not lose a drop of water; R' Yehoshua ben Chanania — his mother deserves praise; R' Yose the *Kohein* is very careful when performing *mitzvos*; R' Shimon ben Nesanel is very careful not to sin; and R' Elazar ben Arach is like a spring of water that flows stronger and stronger."

12. He used to say about his students: "If all the Torah Sages' knowledge were placed on one side of a scale and R' Eliezer ben Hyrkanos' knowledge were placed on the other side, R' Eliezer's would weigh more."

Abba Shaul said that he heard Rabban Yochanan ben Zakkai say: "If all the Torah Sages' brilliance were placed on one side of a scale together with R' Eliezer ben Hyrkanos' brilliance, and R' Elazar's ben Arach's brilliance were placed on the other side, R' Elazar's would weigh more."

רַבִּי אֱלִיעֶזֶר בֶּן הָרְקָנוֹס, בּוֹר סִיד שֶׁאֵינוֹ מְאַבֵּד טִפָּה; רַבִּי יְהוֹשֻׁעַ בֶּן חֲנַנְיָא, אַשְׁרֵי יוֹלַדְתּוֹ; רַבִּי יוֹסֵי הַכֹּהֵן, חָסִיד; רַבִּי שִׁמְעוֹן בֶּן נְתַנְאֵל, יְרֵא חֵטְא; וְרַבִּי אֶלְעָזָר בֶּן עֲרָךְ, כְּמַעְיָן הַמִּתְגַּבֵּר.

[יב] הוּא הָיָה אוֹמֵר: "אִם יִהְיוּ כָּל חַכְמֵי יִשְׂרָאֵל בְּכַף מֹאזְנַיִם, וֶאֱלִיעֶזֶר בֶּן הָרְקָנוֹס בְּכַף שְׁנִיָּה, מַכְרִיעַ אֶת כֻּלָּם."

אַבָּא שָׁאוּל אוֹמֵר מִשְּׁמוֹ: "אִם יִהְיוּ כָּל חַכְמֵי יִשְׂרָאֵל בְּכַף מֹאזְנַיִם, וְרַבִּי אֱלִיעֶזֶר בֶּן הָרְקָנוֹס אַף עִמָּהֶם, וְרַבִּי אֶלְעָזָר בֶּן עֲרָךְ בְּכַף שְׁנִיָּה, מַכְרִיעַ אֶת כֻּלָּם."

we describe how great these *tzaddikim* were, we learn even more.

שֶׁאֵינוֹ מְאַבֵּד טִפָּה — **That does not lose a drop of water.**
Torah is compared to fresh water. R' Eliezer ben Hyrkanos never forgot what he had learned. Therefore he was like a leakproof tank that never loses a drop of water.

אַשְׁרֵי יוֹלַדְתּוֹ — **His mother deserves praise.** Before her son was born, R' Yehoshua's mother would go to every *beis midrash* (study hall) in her city. There, she would ask the rabbis to pray that her child would be a Torah scholar.
After he was born, she would bring his cradle to the *beis*

midrash. She wanted him to become used to the sounds of Torah study, even before he could understand them.

חָסִיד — **Very careful when performing *mitzvos*.**
A חָסִיד, *chassid,* is a person who is so careful when performing *mitzvos* that he will usually do much more than the Torah demands of him.

כְּמַעְיָן הַמִּתְגַּבֵּר — **Like a spring of water that flows stronger and stronger.**
R' Elazar remembered whatever he had learned. And he kept adding more and more original explanations to what his teachers had taught him.

13. Rabban Yochanan ben Zakkai told his students, "Go out and see if you can discover which good path each person should follow."

R' Eliezer said, "Look at everything with a good eye."

[יג] אָמַר לָהֶם: צְאוּ וּרְאוּ אֵיזוֹ הִיא דֶּרֶךְ טוֹבָה שֶׁיִּדְבַּק בָּהּ הָאָדָם. רַבִּי אֱלִיעֶזֶר אוֹמֵר: עַיִן טוֹבָה.

דֶּרֶךְ לֵב טוֹב

R' Yehoshua said, "A good friend."

R' Yose said, "A good neighbor."

R' Shimon said, "Before you do something, think of what it will lead to."

R' Elazar said, "Have a good heart."

Rabban Yochanan then said, "I like Elazar ben Arach's answer better than the others answers, because 'a good heart' contains everything that all of you have said."

14. He then told his students, "Go out and see if you can discover which evil path each person should keep away from."

R' Eliezer said, "Don't look at anything with a bad eye."

R' Yehoshua said, "Don't be a bad friend."

R' Yose said, "Don't be a bad neighbor."

R' Shimon said, "Don't be a person who borrows and then doesn't pay back. Borrowing from another person is like borrowing from Hashem. And we are taught in *Tehillim* (37:21): "A wicked person borrows and does not pay back, but *Hashem* is a *Tzaddik*, He is kind and He gives."

R' Elazar said, "Don't have an evil heart."

Rabban Yochanan then said, "I like Elazar ben Arach's answer better than the other answers, because 'an evil heart' contains everything that all of you have said."

15. Each of Rabban Yochanan's students taught three important lessons. R' Eliezer taught: (a) Your friend's honor should be as important to you as your own, therefore you should not get angry easily. (b) Do *teshuvah* for your sins the day before you die. (c) Warm

רַבִּי יְהוֹשֻׁעַ אוֹמֵר: חָבֵר טוֹב.

רַבִּי יוֹסֵי אוֹמֵר: שָׁכֵן טוֹב.

רַבִּי שִׁמְעוֹן אוֹמֵר: הָרוֹאֶה אֶת הַנּוֹלָד.

רַבִּי אֶלְעָזָר אוֹמֵר: לֵב טוֹב.

אָמַר לָהֶם: רוֹאֶה אֲנִי אֶת דִּבְרֵי אֶלְעָזָר בֶּן עֲרָךְ מִדִּבְרֵיכֶם, שֶׁבִּכְלַל דְּבָרָיו דִּבְרֵיכֶם.

[יד] אָמַר לָהֶם: צְאוּ וּרְאוּ אֵיזוֹ הִיא דֶרֶךְ רָעָה שֶׁיִּתְרַחֵק מִמֶּנָּה הָאָדָם.

רַבִּי אֱלִיעֶזֶר אוֹמֵר: עַיִן רָעָה.

רַבִּי יְהוֹשֻׁעַ אוֹמֵר: חָבֵר רָע.

רַבִּי יוֹסֵי אוֹמֵר: שָׁכֵן רָע.

רַבִּי שִׁמְעוֹן אוֹמֵר: הַלֹּוֶה וְאֵינוֹ מְשַׁלֵּם. אֶחָד הַלֹּוֶה מִן הָאָדָם כְּלֹוֶה מִן הַמָּקוֹם, שֶׁנֶּאֱמַר: "לֹוֶה רָשָׁע וְלֹא יְשַׁלֵּם, וְצַדִּיק חוֹנֵן וְנוֹתֵן".

רַבִּי אֶלְעָזָר אוֹמֵר: לֵב רָע.

אָמַר לָהֶם: רוֹאֶה אֲנִי אֶת דִּבְרֵי אֶלְעָזָר בֶּן עֲרָךְ מִדִּבְרֵיכֶם, שֶׁבִּכְלַל דְּבָרָיו דִּבְרֵיכֶם.

[טו] הֵם אָמְרוּ שְׁלֹשָׁה דְבָרִים. רַבִּי אֱלִיעֶזֶר אוֹמֵר: יְהִי כְבוֹד חֲבֵרְךָ חָבִיב עָלֶיךָ כְּשֶׁלָּךְ, וְאַל תְּהִי נוֹחַ לִכְעֹס; וְשׁוּב יוֹם אֶחָד לִפְנֵי מִיתָתְךָ; וֶהֱוֵי

---

13. חָבֵר טוֹב ... שָׁכֵן טוֹב — **A good friend ... A good neighbor.**

These lessons tell us to choose our friends and neighbors carefully. We learn good things from good people. We learn bad things from bad people. Another thing that these lessons teach is that we must always try to be good friends and good neighbors.

14. לֹוֶה רָשָׁע וְלֹא יְשַׁלֵּם וְצַדִּיק חוֹנֵן וְנוֹתֵן — **A wicked person borrows and does not pay back, but Hashem is a Tzaddik, He is kind and he gives.**

When a wicked man borrows money, he has no intention of ever returning it. But *Hashem* does not want the good lender to lose his money, so He finds a way to return the money. In this way, if a person borrows and does not try to

return what he borrowed, it is as if he took money from *Hashem*.

15. וְשׁוּב — **Do teshuvah.**

Doing *teshuvah* means telling *Hashem* that we are sorry for the sins that we have done, and promising not to repeat them. It also means apologizing to the people whom we have treated badly, and asking them to forgive us.

וְשׁוּב יוֹם אֶחָד לִפְנֵי מִיתָתְךָ — **Do teshuvah for your sins the day before you die.**

When R' Eliezer taught this lesson to his students, they asked him, "But does a person know on which day he will die?"

R' Eliezer answered, "Therefore he must do *teshuvah* every day, for maybe he will die on the next day."

your soul with the fiery words of the Torah Sages, but be careful not to burn yourself with their coals; for their words can bite like a fox, sting like a scorpion, and hiss like a serpent — in fact, all their words are like burning coals.

16. R' Yehoshua taught that three bad things remove a person from this world: A bad eye; the *yetzer hara;* and hating other people.

17. R' Yose taught: (a) Your friend's money should be as important to you as your own. (b) You must prepare yourself to study Torah because you do not learn it by inheritance. (c) Everything you do must be done for *Hashem's* sake.

18. R' Shimon taught: (a) Be very careful about when to recite *Shema* and *Shemoneh Esrei.*

מִתְחַמֵּם כְּנֶגֶד אוּרָן שֶׁל חֲכָמִים, וֶהֱוֵי זָהִיר בְּגַחַלְתָּן שֶׁלֹא תִכָּוֶה — שֶׁנְּשִׁיכָתָן נְשִׁיכַת שׁוּעָל, וַעֲקִיצָתָן עֲקִיצַת עַקְרָב, וּלְחִישָׁתָן לְחִישַׁת שָׂרָף, וְכָל דִּבְרֵיהֶם כְּגַחֲלֵי אֵשׁ.

[טז] רַבִּי יְהוֹשֻׁעַ אוֹמֵר: עַיִן הָרָע, וְיֵצֶר הָרָע, וְשִׂנְאַת הַבְּרִיּוֹת מוֹצִיאִין אֶת הָאָדָם מִן הָעוֹלָם.

[יז] רַבִּי יוֹסֵי אוֹמֵר: יְהִי מָמוֹן חֲבֵרְךָ חָבִיב עָלֶיךָ כְּשֶׁלָּךְ; וְהַתְקֵן עַצְמְךָ לִלְמוֹד תּוֹרָה, שֶׁאֵינָהּ יְרֻשָּׁה לָךְ; וְכָל מַעֲשֶׂיךָ יִהְיוּ לְשֵׁם שָׁמָיִם.

[יח] רַבִּי שִׁמְעוֹן אוֹמֵר: הֱוֵי זָהִיר בִּקְרִיאַת שְׁמַע וּבִתְפִלָּה;

עֶל חֲכָמִים וֶהֱוֵי מִתְחַמֵּם כְּנֶגֶד אוּרָן שֶׁל חֲכָמִים — **Warm your soul with the fiery words of the Torah Sages.**

We should always try to keep close to those who are well learned in Torah. We will hear many good things from them and we will also learn by watching what they do. But we must always be careful to show them great respect and to act properly in their presence. Otherwise they may "burn" us with "flaming" words of *mussar* (rebuke).

16. עַיִן הָרָע וְיֵצֶר הָרָע וְשִׂנְאַת הַבְּרִיּוֹת — **A bad eye; the yetzer hara; and hate for other people.**

"A bad eye" means being jealous of others. "Yetzer hara" means the desire and appetite for things that the Torah tells us not to do. And "hating other people" is caused by a sickness called depression. Someone who is depressed thinks that people don't care about him. So he starts to hate them in return. He will soon begin to hate even himself and will stop taking care of his needs. Jealousy, desire and

depression are three bad things that don't allow a person to live a peaceful life.

17. שֶׁאֵינָהּ יְרֻשָּׁה לָךְ — **You do not learn it by inheritance.**

A *Kohein's* son is a *Kohein,* even though he does nothing to earn this position. A rich man's son may be rich, even though he never worked for a penny in his whole life. But a wise man's son will not become wise unless he spends time and makes an effort to gain wisdom. No matter how much Torah a father studies, no matter how much knowledge he gathers, his sons will not inherit his knowledge, they will not become Torah scholars — unless they prepare themselves with Torah study.

18. הֱוֵי זָהִיר בִּקְרִיאַת שְׁמַע וּבִתְפִלָּה — **Be very careful about when to recite Shema and Shemoneh Esrei.**

Certain *mitzvos* may be done at any time during the day. If one forgets to do them in the morning, he may still do

(b) When you pray, do not pray out of habit, but beg for kindness and mercy from *Hashem;* as the *Navi* (*Yoel* 2:13) teaches, "He is merciful and kind, slow to anger, full of love and forgiving of evil." (c) Do not think of yourself as an evil person.

19. R' Elazar taught:

(a) Put much effort into the study of Torah. (b) Know what to answer to a person who makes fun of the Torah. (c) Know who your *Master* is; and that He can be trusted to pay you for your work.

20. R' Tarfon taught:

The day is short; the job is big; the workers are lazy; the reward is great; and the Master is demanding.

21. He also taught:

(a) You are not expected to finish the job, but you are not free to quit. (b) If you have learned much Torah, you will be given a great reward. (c) Your Master can be trusted to pay you for your work. (d) You should know that a *tzaddik* receives his reward in the World to Come.

וּכְשֶׁאַתָּה מִתְפַּלֵּל, אַל תַּעַשׂ תְּפִלָּתְךָ קֶבַע, אֶלָּא רַחֲמִים וְתַחֲנוּנִים לִפְנֵי הַמָּקוֹם, שֶׁנֶּאֱמַר: "כִּי חַנּוּן וְרַחוּם הוּא אֶרֶךְ אַפַּיִם וְרַב חֶסֶד וְנִחָם עַל הָרָעָה." וְאַל תְּהִי רָשָׁע בִּפְנֵי עַצְמֶךָ.

[יט] רַבִּי אֶלְעָזָר אוֹמֵר: הֱוֵי שָׁקוּד לִלְמוֹד תּוֹרָה. וְדַע מַה שֶׁתָּשִׁיב לְאֶפִּיקוֹרוֹס. וְדַע לִפְנֵי מִי אַתָּה עָמֵל; וְנֶאֱמָן הוּא בַּעַל מְלַאכְתְּךָ, שֶׁיְּשַׁלֵּם לְךָ שְׂכַר פְּעֻלָּתֶךָ.

[כ] רַבִּי טַרְפוֹן אוֹמֵר: הַיּוֹם קָצֵר; וְהַמְּלָאכָה מְרֻבָּה; וְהַפּוֹעֲלִים עֲצֵלִים, וְהַשָּׂכָר הַרְבֵּה; וּבַעַל הַבַּיִת דּוֹחֵק.

[כא] הוּא הָיָה אוֹמֵר: לֹא עָלֶיךָ הַמְּלָאכָה לִגְמוֹר, וְלֹא אַתָּה בֶן חֹרִין לְהִבָּטֵל מִמֶּנָּה. אִם לָמַדְתָּ תּוֹרָה הַרְבֵּה, נוֹתְנִים לְךָ שְׂכַר הַרְבֵּה. וְנֶאֱמָן הוּא בַּעַל מְלַאכְתְּךָ, שֶׁיְּשַׁלֵּם לְךָ שְׂכַר פְּעֻלָּתֶךָ. וְדַע שֶׁמַּתַּן שְׂכָרָן שֶׁל צַדִּיקִים לֶעָתִיד לָבֹא.

---

them in the afternoon. For example, on Purim the *Megillah* must be read once at night and a second time in the morning. If someone did not read (or hear) the *Megillah* early on Purim morning, he may still read it in the afternoon.

But with *Shema* and *Shemoneh Esrei* this is not true. The morning *Shema* must be recited during the first three hours of the day. *Shemoneh Esrei* of *Shacharis* must be recited during the first four hours of the day. Once that time has passed, the *mitzvah* of reciting these prayers at their proper time is lost.

וְאַל תְּהִי רָשָׁע בִּפְנֵי עַצְמֶךָ — Do not think of yourself as an evil person.

Even if someone has sinned many times, he should not think of himself as an evil person. If he thinks of himself as an evil person, he will give up trying to change his ways. He will just get worse and worse. Instead, he should admit that he has done wrong and try to mend his ways. If he thinks of himself as a good person who has made a mistake, he will want to improve himself. And he will succeed.

19. וְדַע מַה שֶׁתָּשִׁיב לְאֶפִּיקוֹרוֹס — Know what to answer to a person who makes fun of the Torah.

Notice that the *mishnah* does not say, "Know what to tell," or, "Know what to ask." When it comes to people who make fun of the Torah, we should keep our distance. We should not start any conversations or arguments with them. However, if they ask us questions, we must be prepared to answer them.

20. הַיּוֹם . . . וְהַמְּלָאכָה . . . — The day . . . the job . . .

"The day" stands for life in this world, which is very short compared to the life in *Olam Haba* (the World to Come).

"The job" is gaining as much knowledge of the Torah and serving *Hashem* by doing His *mitzvos*. It is a big job, for the Torah is endless and the *mitzvos* are many. "The workers," all of us, are lazy when it comes to fulfilling our job. But we must always remember that "the reward" — life in *Olam Haba* — is greater than our greatest dream. And the "Master," *Hashem*, demands that we do our job as best as we can.

21. לֹא עָלֶיךָ הַמְּלָאכָה לִגְמוֹר — You are not expected to finish the job.

As we learned in the last *mishnah*, the job is very big. But even though *Hashem* demands that we do our jobs as best as we can, He does not expect us to complete our jobs. Just the same, we are not free to quit in the middle, but must continue to do our best for as long as we are able.

﷽ CHAPTER THREE / פרק שלישי ﴾

1. **A**kavia ben Mehalalel taught:

Always think about three things, and you will not sin. The three things are:

(a) From where did you come?

(b) To where are you going?

(c) Before whom will you have to explain all of your actions?

[א] **עֲקַבְיָא** בֶּן מַהֲלַלְאֵל אוֹמֵר: הִסְתַּכֵּל בִּשְׁלֹשָׁה דְבָרִים וְאֵין אַתָּה בָא לִידֵי עֲבֵרָה. דַּע — מֵאַיִן בָּאתָ? וּלְאָן אַתָּה הוֹלֵךְ? וְלִפְנֵי מִי אַתָּה עָתִיד לִתֵּן דִּין וְחֶשְׁבּוֹן?

From where did you come? To where are you going?

1. הִסְתַּכֵּל בִּשְׁלֹשָׁה דְבָרִים — **Always think about three things.**

There are three *middos* that cause a person to become sinful. One of these three is גַּאֲוָה, *pride.* A person with too much pride seeks honor and glory for himself. He will do whatever he can to feed his pride — he might even sin.

The second of the three *middos* that lead to sinfulness is תַּאֲוָה, *desire,* a never-satisfied appetite for the most, the biggest, the fanciest, the finest of everything. A person who does not control his desires will do anything to get more and more — he might even steal.

The third of the *middos* that leads to sinfulness is אֶפִּיקוֹרְסוּת, *not believing in Hashem.* If a person puts Hashem out of his mind, nothing will stop him from doing whatever he wants to do. But a person with love and fear of Hashem will always think twice before doing anything. His love of Hashem will cause him to ask, "Is this what Hashem wants me to do? Will what I am doing make Hashem proud of me?" If this doesn't stop him from sinning, then his fear of Hashem will make him think, "If I do something bad, Hashem will punish me."

This *mishnah* tells us how we can keep away the three bad *middos* of גַּאֲוָה, תַּאֲוָה and אֶפִּיקוֹרְסוּת.

The answers to these questions are:

(a) From where did you come? — From a tiny cell that could have easily spoiled.

(b) To where are you going? — To a place of dust, where even tiny worms are stronger than the strongest man.

(c) Before Whom will you have to explain all of your actions? — Before *Hashem*, the King of kings, He is the Holy One, Blessed is He.

2. R' Chanina the assistant *Kohein Gadol* taught:

Pray for the peace of the government, because if people were not afraid of the government, they would swallow each other alive.

3. R' Chanina ben Teradyon taught:

If two people sit together and do not speak any words of Torah, they are like a group of jokers — as it is written in *Tehillim* (1:1-2), "He did not sit in a 'group of jokers,' but he desired *Hashem's* Torah."

However, if two people sit together and do speak words of Torah, then *Hashem's* Presence rests between them — as the *Navi* (*Malachi* 3:16) writes, "When those who fear *Hashem* spoke to one another, *Hashem* listened and heard, and had their words written in a book of remembrance about those who fear *Hashem* and think about Him."

מֵאַיִן בָּאתָ? – מִטִּפָּה סְרוּחָה.
וּלְאָן אַתָּה הוֹלֵךְ? – לִמְקוֹם עָפָר,
רִמָּה וְתוֹלֵעָה.

וְלִפְנֵי מִי אַתָּה עָתִיד לִתֵּן דִּין וְחֶשְׁבּוֹן?
– לִפְנֵי מֶלֶךְ מַלְכֵי הַמְּלָכִים, הַקָּדוֹשׁ
בָּרוּךְ הוּא.

[ב] רַבִּי חֲנִינָא סְגַן הַכֹּהֲנִים אוֹמֵר: הֱוֵי
מִתְפַּלֵּל בִּשְׁלוֹמָהּ שֶׁל מַלְכוּת,
שֶׁאִלְמָלֵא מוֹרָאָהּ, אִישׁ אֶת רֵעֵהוּ חַיִּים
בְּלָעוֹ.

[ג] רַבִּי חֲנִינָא בֶּן תְּרַדְיוֹן אוֹמֵר: שְׁנַיִם
שֶׁיּוֹשְׁבִין וְאֵין בֵּינֵיהֶם דִּבְרֵי תוֹרָה,
הֲרֵי זֶה מוֹשַׁב לֵצִים, שֶׁנֶּאֱמַר: "וּבְמוֹשַׁב
לֵצִים לֹא יָשָׁב..."

אֲבָל שְׁנַיִם שֶׁיּוֹשְׁבִין וְיֵשׁ בֵּינֵיהֶם דִּבְרֵי
תוֹרָה, שְׁכִינָה שְׁרוּיָה בֵינֵיהֶם – שֶׁנֶּאֱמַר,
"אָז נִדְבְּרוּ יִרְאֵי ה' אִישׁ אֶל רֵעֵהוּ,
וַיַּקְשֵׁב ה' וַיִּשְׁמָע, וַיִּכָּתֵב סֵפֶר זִכָּרוֹן
לְפָנָיו, לְיִרְאֵי ה' וּלְחֹשְׁבֵי שְׁמוֹ."

מִטִּפָּה סְרוּחָה — **From a tiny cell that could have easily spoiled.**

Before a baby is born, it begins as a tiny cell, as small as the point of a pin. For nine months that cell grows and grows until it become a full-sized baby. But if *Hashem* didn't allow this tiny cell to begin growing, it would have spoiled and melted away.

A person should always remember that he was once just a tiny cell that could have easily spoiled. If he thinks this way, he will never be guilty of too much pride.

לִמְקוֹם עָפָר רִמָּה וְתוֹלֵעָה — **To a place of dust, where even tiny worms are stronger than the strongest man.**

A person does not live forever. He is like a traveler going from place to place. A traveler does not bring his furniture and all of his finery with him when he travels. A suitcase or two is all he takes with him. He must learn to be satisfied with a little.

When a person goes on to his new life, his fancy house and car do not go with him. He must leave behind all of his beautiful clothing and elegant furniture. His servants and maids do not accompany him. The only luggage he can take along is his *mitzvos* and good deeds.

A person who thinks this way will be saved from תַּאֲוָה,

and from all the sinfulness that it can lead to.

לִפְנֵי מֶלֶךְ מַלְכֵי הַמְּלָכִים — **Before Hashem, the King of kings.**

Finally, a person who always remembers that he will stand in judgment before *Hashem* will carefully consider everything he does. This will prevent him from sinning. And, even more, it will cause him to seek *mitzvos*. This is why David *Hamelech* (King David) taught us, "שִׁוִּיתִי ה' לְנֶגְדִּי תָמִיד, I always have placed *Hashem* in front of me" (*Tehillim* 16:8).

2. אִישׁ אֶת רֵעֵהוּ חַיִּים בְּלָעוֹ — **They would swallow each other alive.**

The government keeps things in order and peaceful. People, who otherwise might commit crime, don't, because they are afraid that the government's police force will catch them and punish them.

The *Gemara* (*Avodah Zarah* 4b) teaches that without government people would act like fish. In the sea there are no policemen. Any fish can do whatever he wants to. And so, larger fish swallow up smaller fish. Then the larger fish are swallowed up by even larger ones. If there were no government to control people, they would act the same way. The stronger person would take everything away from the weaker person, until an even stronger person would come along and take everything away from him.

... written in a book of remembrance ...

Now you may ask, "This lesson only teaches us about two people who discuss the Torah. How do we know that *Hashem* gives a reward even to one person who sits by himself and studies Torah?"

The answer to this question is found in *Megillas Eichah* (3:28), "Although he sits alone and studies in silence, he will receive a reward for what he does."

4. R' Shimon taught:

If three people ate at one table and they did not speak any words of Torah, it is as if they ate the sacrifices of dead idols — as the *Navi (Yeshayahu 28:8)* writes: "For all the tables are full of vomit and filth, when *Hashem* is not mentioned."

אֵין לִי אֶלָּא שְׁנַיִם; מִנַּיִן שֶׁאֲפִילוּ אֶחָד שֶׁיוֹשֵׁב וְעוֹסֵק בַּתּוֹרָה, שֶׁהַקָּדוֹשׁ בָּרוּךְ הוּא קוֹבֵעַ לוֹ שָׂכָר?
שֶׁנֶּאֱמַר: "יֵשֵׁב בָּדָד וְיִדֹּם, כִּי נָטַל עָלָיו."

[ד] רַבִּי שִׁמְעוֹן אוֹמֵר: שְׁלשָׁה שֶׁאָכְלוּ עַל שֻׁלְחָן אֶחָד וְלֹא אָמְרוּ עָלָיו דִּבְרֵי תוֹרָה, כְּאִלּוּ אָכְלוּ מִזִּבְחֵי מֵתִים, שֶׁנֶּאֱמַר: "כִּי כָּל שֻׁלְחָנוֹת מָלְאוּ קִיא צוֹאָה, בְּלִי מָקוֹם."

---

4. קִיא צוֹאָה — **Vomit and filth.**
This is how the *Navi* describes idols.

מָקוֹם — **Hashem.**
God is often called הַמָּקוֹם which means "The Place." This

is because God is in every possible place. There is no place in the world without Him. In fact, He is even bigger than the world. This is why the *Midrash* calls *Hashem* the Place of the world.

. . . and they did speak words of Torah . . .

However, if three people ate at one table and they did speak words of Torah there, it is as if they ate from *Hashem's* table — as the *Navi (Yechezkel* 4:22) writes: "And he spoke of Me; this is the table that is before *Hashem*."

אֲבָל שְׁלשָׁה שֶׁאָכְלוּ עַל שֻׁלְחָן אֶחָד וְאָמְרוּ עָלָיו דִּבְרֵי תוֹרָה, כְּאִלּוּ אָכְלוּ מִשֻּׁלְחָנוֹ שֶׁל מָקוֹם, שֶׁנֶּאֱמַר: ,,וַיְדַבֵּר אֵלַי, זֶה הַשֻּׁלְחָן אֲשֶׁר לִפְנֵי ה׳.''

5. R' Chanina ben Chachinai taught:

If a person is awake at night or travels alone on the road, and turns his heart to worthless thoughts, then he can blame only himself if anything bad happens to him.

6. R' Nechunia ben Hakanah taught:

Any person who accepts the yoke of Torah, will be excused from the yoke of the government and from the yoke of a job.

However, any person who removes the yoke of Torah from himself will have the yoke of the government and the yoke of a job placed upon him.

7. R' Chalafta ben Dosa of Kfar Chanania taught:

If ten people sit together studying the Torah, then *Hashem's* Presence rests among them — as it is written in *Tehillim* (82:1), "God stands in the *minyan* of *tzaddikim* who are strong in the Torah's ways."

How do we know that *Hashem* joins even five people who study Torah together? The *Navi* (*Amos* 9:6) writes, "He, God, has set up His bundle upon earth."

How do we know that *Hashem* joins even three people who study Torah together? It is written in *Tehillim* (82:1), "He, God, judges together with the judges of the *beis din*."

[ה] רַבִּי חֲנִינָא בֶּן חֲכִינַאי אוֹמֵר: הַנֵּעוֹר בַּלַּיְלָה, וְהַמְהַלֵּךְ בַּדֶּרֶךְ יְחִידִי, וּמְפַנֶּה לִבּוֹ לְבַטָּלָה — הֲרֵי זֶה מִתְחַיֵּב בְּנַפְשׁוֹ.

[ו] רַבִּי נְחוּנְיָא בֶּן הַקָּנָה אוֹמֵר: כָּל הַמְקַבֵּל עָלָיו עֹל תּוֹרָה, מַעֲבִירִין מִמֶּנּוּ עֹל מַלְכוּת וְעֹל דֶּרֶךְ אֶרֶץ; וְכָל הַפּוֹרֵק מִמֶּנּוּ עֹל תּוֹרָה, נוֹתְנִין עָלָיו עֹל מַלְכוּת וְעֹל דֶּרֶךְ אֶרֶץ.

[ז] רַבִּי חֲלַפְתָּא בֶּן דּוֹסָא אִישׁ כְּפַר חֲנַנְיָא אוֹמֵר: עֲשָׂרָה שֶׁיּוֹשְׁבִין וְעוֹסְקִין בַּתּוֹרָה, שְׁכִינָה שְׁרוּיָה בֵּינֵיהֶם, שֶׁנֶּאֱמַר, "אֱלֹהִים נִצָּב בַּעֲדַת אֵל." וּמִנַּיִן אֲפִילוּ חֲמִשָּׁה? שֶׁנֶּאֱמַר, "וַאֲגֻדָּתוֹ עַל אֶרֶץ יְסָדָהּ." וּמִנַּיִן אֲפִילוּ שְׁלֹשָׁה? שֶׁנֶּאֱמַר, "בְּקֶרֶב אֱלֹהִים יִשְׁפֹּט."

---

5. הֲרֵי זֶה מִתְחַיֵּב בְּנַפְשׁוֹ — **He can blame only himself if anything bad happens to him.**

Torah study and thoughts about Torah protect a person from two types of harm. First, when someone speaks and thinks words of Torah, he creates *malachim* (angels) that watch over him. Second, a mind filled with Torah does not have room for sinful thoughts.

Night time is usually peaceful and quiet. It is a wonderful time to concentrate on Torah study without being interrupted. Someone who wastes such precious time by filling his mind with nonsense, may soon find his head full of sinful thoughts.

All roads present some sort of danger — drunk drivers, broken pavement, wild animals. That is why *Hashem* sends His *malachim* to accompany a traveler, as it is written in *Tehillim* (91:11), "*Hashem* will command His angels for you, to protect you in all your ways." These *malachim* are created by the Torah that a person studies. If a person travels alone, he places himself in danger. If he thinks Torah thoughts, he protects himself.

6. עֹל תּוֹרָה . . . עֹל מַלְכוּת וְעֹל דֶּרֶךְ אֶרֶץ — **The yoke of Torah . . . the yoke of the government and the yoke of a job.**

Accepting the "yoke of Torah" means dedicating every possible moment to the study of Torah. The "yoke of the government" refers to the oppressive and harsh demands that some governments make on their people. The "yoke of

a job" is a person's responsibility to work at a job in order to earn enough money to support himself and his family.

One who accepts the yoke of Torah is freed from the other two burdens. As we will learn later (chapter 6, *mishnah* 2), "There is no truly free man, except one who devotes himself to the study of Torah." This means that even if the person must hold a job to support his family, he should make a super-human effort to study Torah whenever he can. In return, *Hashem* will supply his needs in a super-natural way. The more time a man dedicates to Torah study, the less effort he will have to spend on earning a living. The same is true about the "yoke of government," because *Hashem* will protect him against its harshness.

7. חֲמִשָּׁה . . . וַאֲגֻדָּתוֹ — **Five . . . His bundle.**

An אֲגֻדָּה is a bundle carried in one hand. Therefore the word אֲגֻדָּה is sometimes used to described the five fingers of one hand. *Hashem's* "bundle" means a group of five people studying Torah together.

שְׁלֹשָׁה . . . אֱלֹהִים — **Three . . . the judges of the beis din.**

The word אֱלֹהִים usually means God. But sometimes it means judges, especially the judges of a *beis din*, as a Torah court is called. And a *beis din* usually has three judges. So this verse teaches us that when the judges (three people) are deciding the Torah law (and speaking words of Torah), *Hashem* joins them.

How do we know that *Hashem* joins even two people who study Torah together? The *Navi* (Malachi 3:16) writes, "When those who fear *Hashem* spoke to one another, *Hashem* listened and heard."

And how do we know that *Hashem* joins even one person who studies Torah by himself? It is written in the Torah (Shemos 20:21), "In every place where I have My Name mentioned, I will come to you and bless you."

8. R' Elazar of Bartosa taught:

Spend money for mitzvos and you will be giving *Hashem* what belongs to Him; because you and all that you own belong to Him. This is what David *Hamelech* meant when he said (I Divrei Hayamim 29:14), "Everything comes from You, and whatever we have given You comes from Your hand."

9. R' Yaakov taught:

If someone travels on the road reviewing his Torah lessons, but stops his review and says, "What a beautiful tree this is!" or, "What a beautiful field this is!" the Torah teaches that he can blame only himself if bad things happen to him.

וּמִנַּיִן אֲפִילוּ שְׁנַיִם? שֶׁנֶּאֱמַר, "אָז נִדְבְּרוּ יִרְאֵי ה' אִישׁ אֶל רֵעֵהוּ וַיַּקְשֵׁב ה' וַיִּשְׁמָע".

וּמִנַּיִן אֲפִילוּ אֶחָד? שֶׁנֶּאֱמַר: "בְּכָל הַמָּקוֹם אֲשֶׁר אַזְכִּיר אֶת שְׁמִי, אָבוֹא אֵלֶיךָ וּבֵרַכְתִּיךָ".

[ח] רַבִּי אֶלְעָזָר אִישׁ בַּרְתּוֹתָא אוֹמֵר: תֶּן לוֹ מִשֶּׁלּוֹ, שֶׁאַתָּה וְשֶׁלְּךָ שֶׁלּוֹ; וְכֵן בְּדָוִד הוּא אוֹמֵר: "כִּי מִמְּךָ הַכֹּל, וּמִיָּדְךָ נָתַנּוּ לָךְ".

[ט] רַבִּי יַעֲקֹב אוֹמֵר: הַמְהַלֵּךְ בַּדֶּרֶךְ וְשׁוֹנֶה, וּמַפְסִיק מִמִּשְׁנָתוֹ, וְאוֹמֵר: "מַה נָּאֶה אִילָן זֶה וּמַה נָּאֶה נִיר זֶה" — מַעֲלֶה עָלָיו הַכָּתוּב כְּאִלּוּ מִתְחַיֵּב בְּנַפְשׁוֹ.

אֲפִילוּ שְׁנַיִם . . . אֲפִילוּ אֶחָד — Even two . . . even one.

The *mishnah* teaches us that whenever someone studies Torah, *Hashem* comes to join in. So why does the *mishnah* first speak of ten, then five, then three, two and one? This teaches us that the more people that learn Torah together, the better.

8. רַבִּי אֶלְעָזָר אִישׁ בַּרְתּוֹתָא — R' Elazar of Bartosa.

This *Tanna* was well known as a very charitable man. The *Gemara* (Taanis 24a) says that he used to give much more money than he should have. In fact, whenever the town's official *tzedakah gabbaim* (charity collectors) saw him coming, they would hide. They were afraid that he would give them every cent that he had.

One day, R' Elazar was on his way to the market to buy whatever he needed for his daughter's wedding. The *gabbaim* saw him and ran to hide, but it was too late. He had spotted them first. He ran after them. When he caught up with them, he asked, "For what are you collecting?"

They said, "There is a poor orphan boy who is engaged to a poor orphan girl. They have no money for their wedding."

"How much money do you still need?" R' Elazar asked. When they told him the amount, he said, "Why I just happen to have that much with me. Here, take it. The two orphans are much more important than my daughter."

Now R' Elazar had given them almost all the money he had. Only one coin remained. With that coin he bought a small amount of wheat. When he came home, he placed the wheat in his grain crib.

His daughter saw him and said, "Father, what have you bought for my wedding?"

He answered, "Whatever you find in the grain crib." Then he went to the *beis midrash* to study.

R' Elazar's daughter walked sadly to the grain crib. "All I have for my wedding is a few pieces of wheat," she thought.

Imagine how surprised she was when she saw the grain crib overflowing with wheat. *Hashem* had made a miracle to repay R' Elazar for the kindness he has shown to the two orphans.

When she saw all the wheat, she ran to the *beis midrash* to tell her father. He said, "We will sell the wheat. But we will only take enough of the money to pay for your wedding expenses. That is the amount we would give any poor girl who came to us for help in making her wedding. Any money that is left over we will give to poor people."

From this story we can understand what R' Elazar meant by, "You and all that you own belong to Him."

9. מַה נָּאֶה אִילָן זֶה — "What a beautiful tree this is!"

When a person sees something beautiful, he praises *Hashem* for creating such beauty in His world. But if someone is studying Torah, he should not stop to look at the beautiful things around him. A person who travels on the road places himself in a dangerous situation. If he reviews his Torah studies while traveling, he creates *malachim* (angels) who protect him from danger — as we discussed in *mishnah* 5. But if he stops his Torah study to talk about the tree, then he loses his protection. If anything bad happens to him, he has only himself to blame.

10. R' Dostai bar Yannai taught this lesson that he learned from R' Meir:

Any person who forgets a part of his Torah learning can blame only himself if bad things happen to him. This is what the Torah means by the sentence *(Devarim* 4:9), ''Just beware! Watch your soul very carefully! Do not forget those things that your eyes have seen!''

Is this true even if the lesson was too difficult for him to remember? No, it does not apply to a very difficult lesson, as the same Torah sentence continues, ''And do not remove them from your heart all the days of your life.'' From this sentence we see that a person is only responsible if he sits by lazily and does not review his lessons. Then he is to blame for forgetting them.

11. R' Chanina ben Dosa taught:

Anyone whose fear of sin is more important to him than his wisdom, his wisdom will remain with him. But anyone whose wisdom is more important to him than his fear of sin, his wisdom will not remain with him.

12. He also taught:

Anyone whose deeds are greater than his wisdom, his wisdom will remain with him. But anyone whose wisdom is greater than his deeds, his wisdom will not remain with him.

13. He also taught:

Anyone who is pleasing to other people, is pleasing also to God. And anyone who is not pleasing to other people, is not pleasing to God.

14. R' Dosa ben Harkinas taught:

Sleeping late in the morning, drinking wine in the afternoon, chattering childishly, and sitting in gatherings of ignorant people — all of these remove a person from the world.

[י] רַבִּי דוֹסְתָּאִי בַּר יַנַּאי מִשּׁוּם רַבִּי מֵאִיר אוֹמֵר: כָּל הַשּׁוֹכֵחַ דָּבָר אֶחָד מִמִּשְׁנָתוֹ, מַעֲלֶה עָלָיו הַכָּתוּב כְּאִלּוּ מִתְחַיֵּב בְּנַפְשׁוֹ. שֶׁנֶּאֱמַר, "רַק הִשָּׁמֶר לְךָ, וּשְׁמֹר נַפְשְׁךָ מְאֹד, פֶּן תִּשְׁכַּח אֶת הַדְּבָרִים אֲשֶׁר רָאוּ עֵינֶיךָ." יָכוֹל אֲפִילוּ תָקְפָה עָלָיו מִשְׁנָתוֹ? תַּלְמוּד לוֹמַר, "וּפֶן יָסוּרוּ מִלְּבָבְךָ כֹּל יְמֵי חַיֶּיךָ." הָא אֵינוֹ מִתְחַיֵּב בְּנַפְשׁוֹ עַד שֶׁיֵּשֵׁב וִיסִירֵם מִלִּבּוֹ.

[יא] רַבִּי חֲנִינָא בֶּן דּוֹסָא אוֹמֵר: כָּל שֶׁיִּרְאַת חֶטְאוֹ קוֹדֶמֶת לְחָכְמָתוֹ, חָכְמָתוֹ מִתְקַיֶּמֶת. וְכָל שֶׁחָכְמָתוֹ קוֹדֶמֶת לְיִרְאַת חֶטְאוֹ, אֵין חָכְמָתוֹ מִתְקַיֶּמֶת.

[יב] הוּא הָיָה אוֹמֵר: כָּל שֶׁמַּעֲשָׂיו מְרֻבִּין מֵחָכְמָתוֹ, חָכְמָתוֹ מִתְקַיֶּמֶת. וְכָל שֶׁחָכְמָתוֹ מְרֻבָּה מִמַּעֲשָׂיו, אֵין חָכְמָתוֹ מִתְקַיֶּמֶת.

[יג] הוּא הָיָה אוֹמֵר: כָּל שֶׁרוּחַ הַבְּרִיּוֹת נוֹחָה הֵימֶנּוּ, רוּחַ הַמָּקוֹם נוֹחָה הֵימֶנּוּ. וְכָל שֶׁאֵין רוּחַ הַבְּרִיּוֹת נוֹחָה הֵימֶנּוּ, אֵין רוּחַ הַמָּקוֹם נוֹחָה הֵימֶנּוּ.

[יד] רַבִּי דוֹסָא בֶּן הָרְכִּינַס אוֹמֵר: שֵׁנָה שֶׁל שַׁחֲרִית, וְיַיִן שֶׁל צָהֳרַיִם, וְשִׂיחַת הַיְלָדִים, וִישִׁיבַת בָּתֵּי כְנֵסִיּוֹת שֶׁל עַמֵּי הָאָרֶץ — מוֹצִיאִין אֶת הָאָדָם מִן הָעוֹלָם.

11-12. ... כָּל שֶׁיִּרְאַת חֶטְאוֹ ... כָּל שֶׁמַּעֲשָׂיו — **Anyone whose fear of sin . . . Anyone whose deeds.**

A person should study Torah in order to know how to perform *mitzvos* and how to keep away from sin. If someone does this, his Torah knowledge will remain with him, because he will always practice what he studies.

But if someone doesn't practice the Torah laws that he studies, he will soon stop studying. And he will lose whatever Torah wisdom he has gained.

Mishnah 11 and *mishnah* 12 teach almost the same lesson; except that *mishnah* 11 speaks about not sinning, while *mishnah* 12 speaks about doing *mitzvos*.

14. שֵׁנָה שֶׁל שַׁחֲרִית — **Sleeping late in the morning.**

Earlier (chapter 2, *Mishnah* 18) we learned that we must always be careful to recite the *Shema* and *Shemoneh Esrei* at their proper times. Our *mishnah* now tells us how bad it is to oversleep these times.

מוֹצִיאִין אֶת הָאָדָם מִן הָעוֹלָם — **Remove a person from the world.**

The activities listed in this *Mishnah* are all ways of wasting precious time. They stop us from doing the things we were created to do.

15. R' Elazar Hamodai taught:

Someone who treats holy things without respect, or who treats *Yomim Tovim* (Festivals) as weekdays, or who shames another person in public, or who denies the holiness of the *mitzvah* of *bris milah* (circumcision) that *Hashem* taught to Avraham *Avinu*, or who explains the Torah in a way that is against *halachah* — even if he has Torah knowledge and good deeds, that person has no share in the World to Come.

16. R' Yishmael taught:

You should be ready to serve an elderly wise man, be nice to a younger person, and greet everybody with joy.

17. R' Akiva taught:

Joking and making fun lead a person to sinfulness.

The Unwritten Torah is a fence that protects the Written Torah.

Separating *maaser* from your crop is a fence that protects your wealth.

Promises are a fence that protects you from the desire for unnecessary things.

The fence that protects wisdom is silence.

[טו] רַבִּי אֶלְעָזָר הַמּוֹדָעִי אוֹמֵר: הַמְחַלֵּל אֶת הַקֳּדָשִׁים, וְהַמְבַזֶּה אֶת הַמּוֹעֲדוֹת, וְהַמַּלְבִּין פְּנֵי חֲבֵרוֹ בָּרַבִּים, וְהַמֵּפֵר בְּרִיתוֹ שֶׁל אַבְרָהָם אָבִינוּ, וְהַמְגַלֶּה פָנִים בַּתּוֹרָה שֶׁלֹּא כַהֲלָכָה, אַף עַל פִּי שֶׁיֵּשׁ בְּיָדוֹ תוֹרָה וּמַעֲשִׂים טוֹבִים — אֵין לוֹ חֵלֶק לָעוֹלָם הַבָּא.

[טז] רַבִּי יִשְׁמָעֵאל אוֹמֵר: הֱוֵי קַל לְרֹאשׁ, וְנוֹחַ לְתִשְׁחֹרֶת, וֶהֱוֵי מְקַבֵּל אֶת כָּל הָאָדָם בְּשִׂמְחָה.

[יז] רַבִּי עֲקִיבָא אוֹמֵר: שְׂחוֹק וְקַלּוּת רֹאשׁ מַרְגִּילִין אֶת הָאָדָם לְעֶרְוָה. מָסוֹרֶת סְיָג לַתּוֹרָה. מַעַשְׂרוֹת סְיָג לָעֹשֶׁר. נְדָרִים סְיָג לַפְּרִישׁוּת. סְיָג לַחָכְמָה שְׁתִיקָה.

---

15. ... הַמְחַלֵּל אֶת הַקֳּדָשִׁים — **Someone who treats holy things without respect . . .**

Hashem created the world and placed many kinds of holiness into it. There is **the holiness of place** — for example, the *Beis Hamikdash* and the *korbanos* (sacrifices) offered there — the *mishnah* calls these קֳדָשִׁים, holy things; **the holiness of time** — such as *Yomim Tovim*; **the holiness of human beings** — the *neshamah* (soul); **the holiness of the Jewish People** — the *bris milah*; and the most holy thing in the whole world — **the holiness of the Torah.**

Anyone who treats holy places, holy days, the Torah, or even other people improperly, shows that he has no respect for *Hashem* and the things that *Hashem* considers special. Such a person does not deserve a share in *Olam Haba* (the World to Come), even if he has studied Torah and done good deeds during his lifetime.

17. שְׂחוֹק וְקַלּוּת רֹאשׁ — **Joking and making fun.**

The *mishnah* speaks of a person who is never serious. He spends his entire day laughing and fooling around. Since he thinks of life as a big joke, he will soon lose respect even for himself. Because of this he will lead himself to sinful ways.

מָסוֹרֶת — **The Unwritten Torah.**

When *Hashem* taught Moshe *Rabbeinu* (our teacher Moses) the Torah at Mount Sinai, He taught him the words as they are written in the *Sefer Torah* (Torah Scroll). But He also explained the meaning of these words to Moshe. The words of the Torah are called תּוֹרָה שֶׁבִּכְתָב, the Written Torah. The explanations are called תּוֹרָה שֶׁבְּעַל פֶּה, the

Unwritten (or Oral) Torah. Without the Unwritten Torah we would never be able to understand the Written Torah.

For many hundreds of years the Unwritten Torah was taught from memory. Each father taught his sons and each teacher taught his students by heart. Many hours were spent each day memorizing the explanations of the Written Torah. This method of passing the teachings of the Unwritten Torah from one generation to the next is called מָסוֹרֶת, *masores*, which means "handing down" or "tradition". This way of learning Torah could only continue as long as the Jewish people were living in freedom in *Eretz Yisrael*.

But during the time of the Second *Beis Hamikdash*, enemy armies conquered the land. These armies demanded heavy taxes. The people had to work long hours in order to pay these taxes. Soon they had very little time left for Torah study. And they began forgetting what they had learned.

About one hundred years after the Second *Beis Hamikdash* was destroyed, R' Yehudah Hanassi saw that all of the Unwritten Torah would soon be forgotten. He gathered together many of the remaining Torah scholars and, with their help, collected the explanations and lessons of the Unwritten Torah that they had been taught by their teachers. They wrote down these lessons and called them *Mishnah*, which means "teaching."

As time went on, more and more of the Unwritten Torah was written down. This second collection of teachings is called the *Gemara* or the *Talmud*. Other parts were written down and called *Midrash*.

The only way we can be sure that we understand the

Maaser is a fence that protects your wealth.

Written Torah is by carefully studying the *Mishnah, Gemara* and *Midrash*. Or, in other words, the תּוֹרָה שֶׁבְּעַל פֶּה is a fence that protects the תּוֹרָה שֶׁבִּכְתָב.

It is interesting to note that the *gematria*, or letter value, of the words בְּעַל פֶּה is 187 (2 + 70 + 30 + 80 + 5), and the *gematria* of בִּכְתָב is 424 (2 + 20 + 400 + 2). Together (187 + 424) these equal 611, the same *gematria* as תּוֹרָה (400 + 6 + 200 + 5).

מַעְשְׂרוֹת סְיָג לְעשֶׁר — **Separating maaser from your crop is a fence to protect your wealth.**

The Torah teaches that the road to riches is open to the person who gives *maaser* (see chapter 1, *mishnah* 16). By giving *maaser*, a person proves that he knows from where his crop came. He shows that all wealth really comes from God, the true Owner of everything in the world. This man deserves to be rich, because he uses his riches to serve God.

18. He also taught:

God loves man, that is why He created him in His own image. God showed Man even greater love by telling Man that God created him in His own image, as the Torah (*Bereishis* 9:6) says, "In the image of God, He made Man."

God loves the Jewish People, that is why they are called "God's children." God showed them even more love by telling them that they are called God's children, as it is written in the Torah (*Devarim* 14:1), "You are the children of *Hashem*, your God."

God loves the Jewish People, that is why He gave them a valuable present, the Torah. God showed them even more love by telling them that He gave them a valuable present, as it is written (*Mishlei* 4:2), "I have given you a good present, do not go away from My Torah."

19. Everything that a person does is seen, yet everyone is permitted to do what he wants to do.

The world is judged in a good way, everything according to how many good deeds a person has done.

20. He also taught that *Hashem* runs the world like a business:

Everything is given on trust, but this can be like a net spread to trap a person. The shop is open; the Storekeeper gives credit; the record book is open; the hand writes; and whoever wants to borrow may come and borrow. But one must remember that the collectors always make their collection rounds, whether the borrower knows about them or not; and they have good proof of what is owed. The judgment is truthful. And everything is prepared for the banquet.

[יח] הוּא הָיָה אוֹמֵר: חָבִיב אָדָם שֶׁנִּבְרָא בְּצֶלֶם. חִבָּה יְתֵרָה נוֹדַעַת לוֹ שֶׁנִּבְרָא בְּצֶלֶם, שֶׁנֶּאֱמַר, "כִּי בְּצֶלֶם אֱלֹהִים עָשָׂה אֶת הָאָדָם."

חֲבִיבִין יִשְׂרָאֵל, שֶׁנִּקְרְאוּ בָנִים לַמָּקוֹם. חִבָּה יְתֵרָה נוֹדַעַת לָהֶם שֶׁנִּקְרְאוּ בָנִים לַמָּקוֹם, שֶׁנֶּאֱמַר, "בָּנִים אַתֶּם לַה' אֱלֹהֵיכֶם."

חֲבִיבִין יִשְׂרָאֵל, שֶׁנִּתַּן לָהֶם כְּלִי חֶמְדָּה. חִבָּה יְתֵרָה נוֹדַעַת לָהֶם, שֶׁנִּתַּן לָהֶם כְּלִי חֶמְדָּה, שֶׁנֶּאֱמַר, "כִּי לֶקַח טוֹב נָתַתִּי לָכֶם, תּוֹרָתִי אַל תַּעֲזֹבוּ."

[יט] הַכֹּל צָפוּי, וְהָרְשׁוּת נְתוּנָה. וּבְטוֹב הָעוֹלָם נָדוֹן, וְהַכֹּל לְפִי רֹב הַמַּעֲשֶׂה.

[כ] הוּא הָיָה אוֹמֵר: הַכֹּל נָתוּן בָּעֵרָבוֹן, וּמְצוּדָה פְרוּסָה עַל כָּל הַחַיִּים. הֶחָנוּת פְּתוּחָה; וְהַחֶנְוָנִי מַקִּיף; וְהַפִּנְקָס פָּתוּחַ; וְהַיָּד כּוֹתֶבֶת; וְכָל הָרוֹצֶה לִלְווֹת יָבֹא וְיִלְוֶה. וְהַגַּבָּאִים מַחֲזִירִין תָּדִיר בְּכָל יוֹם וְנִפְרָעִין מִן הָאָדָם, מִדַּעְתּוֹ וְשֶׁלֹּא מִדַּעְתּוֹ; וְיֵשׁ לָהֶם עַל מַה שֶּׁיִּסְמְכוּ. וְהַדִּין דִּין אֱמֶת. וְהַכֹּל מְתֻקָּן לִסְעוּדָה.

---

18. חִבָּה יְתֵרָה — **Even greater love.**

When you do a favor for another person, you show that you love that person. But if the other person does not know about the favor, he will not be able to share your love.

When you do a favor for another person and you let him know what you have done, you show even more love for that person, because now he will be able to share your love.

19. הַכֹּל צָפוּי וְהָרְשׁוּת נְתוּנָה — **Everything that a person does is seen, yet everyone is permitted to do what he wants to do.**

We have learned at the beginning of chapter 2, that "An Eye sees and an Ear hears" everything that we do or say. Yet this does not force us to do the right thing. Everyone is free to do whatever he wants, whether it is right or wrong, good or bad. But you also must remember (as we have learned at the beginning of this chapter) "before Whom you will have to explain all of your actions." And you will be judged according to those actions.

20. . . . הַכֹּל נָתוּן בָּעֵרָבוֹן — **Everything is given on trust . . .**

Whatever a person owns has been lent to him by *Hashem*. If he forgets the true Owner, then he will fall into "the trap" that will lead to pain and even death.

The "store," that is, the world, is open and full of many different items. The "Storekeeper," *Hashem*, lets everyone take what he wants. But the record book is open and each person's deeds are being written down. And "the collectors" always go around to punish those who do not fulfill their part of the trust. Yet, in the end, even those who were punished will join in "the banquet" of the World to Come, in reward for their good deeds.

21. R' Elazar ben Azaryah taught:

Without Torah, a person cannot do his job honestly; without a job, he cannot learn Torah.

Without wisdom, a person cannot fear God; without fear of God, he cannot become wise.

Without knowledge, a person cannot understand things on his own; without understanding, he cannot gain knowledge.

Without food, a person cannot learn Torah; without Torah, what purpose does his food have?

22. He also taught:

Anyone whose wisdom is greater than his deeds — what is he like? He is like a tree with many branches and few roots. When the wind blows, it will uproot the tree and turn it upside-down. This is what the *Navi* (*Yirmiyahu* 17:6) said, "He will be like a single tree in a dry land; he will not notice when good times come along. He will live on parched soil in the desert, a salty land where no people live."

But anyone whose deeds are greater than his wisdom — what is he like? He is like a tree with few branches and many roots. Even when all the winds in the world blow against it, they will not move it from its place. This is what the *Navi* (*Yirmiyahu* 17:8) said, "He will be like a tree planted near the water, with its roots spreading toward the stream. It will not notice when hot weather comes along, its leaves will remain fresh. In a rainless year it will not worry; and it will not stop giving fruit."

23. R' Elazar ben Chisma taught:

The rules about bird offerings and about husband and wife relationships are among the most important Torah laws. But astronomy and mathematics are only introductions to wisdom.

[כא] רַבִּי אֶלְעָזָר בֶּן עֲזַרְיָה אוֹמֵר: אִם אֵין תּוֹרָה, אֵין דֶּרֶךְ אֶרֶץ; אִם אֵין דֶּרֶךְ אֶרֶץ, אֵין תּוֹרָה. אִם אֵין חָכְמָה, אֵין יִרְאָה; אִם אֵין יִרְאָה, אֵין חָכְמָה. אִם אֵין דַּעַת, אֵין בִּינָה; אִם אֵין בִּינָה, אֵין דַּעַת. אִם אֵין קֶמַח, אֵין תּוֹרָה; אִם אֵין תּוֹרָה, אֵין קֶמַח.

[כב] הוּא הָיָה אוֹמֵר: כֹּל שֶׁחָכְמָתוֹ מְרֻבָּה מִמַּעֲשָׂיו — לְמָה הוּא דוֹמֶה? לְאִילָן שֶׁעֲנָפָיו מְרֻבִּין וְשָׁרָשָׁיו מוּעָטִין. וְהָרוּחַ בָּאָה, וְעוֹקַרְתּוֹ וְהוֹפַכְתּוֹ עַל פָּנָיו. שֶׁנֶּאֱמַר, "וְהָיָה כְּעַרְעָר בָּעֲרָבָה; וְלֹא יִרְאֶה כִּי יָבוֹא טוֹב. וְשָׁכַן חֲרֵרִים בַּמִּדְבָּר, אֶרֶץ מְלֵחָה וְלֹא תֵשֵׁב."

אֲבָל כֹּל שֶׁמַּעֲשָׂיו מְרֻבִּין מֵחָכְמָתוֹ — לְמָה הוּא דוֹמֶה? לְאִילָן שֶׁעֲנָפָיו מוּעָטִין וְשָׁרָשָׁיו מְרֻבִּין. שֶׁאֲפִילוּ כָּל הָרוּחוֹת שֶׁבָּעוֹלָם בָּאוֹת וְנוֹשְׁבוֹת בּוֹ, אֵין מְזִיזִין אוֹתוֹ מִמְּקוֹמוֹ. שֶׁנֶּאֱמַר: "וְהָיָה כְּעֵץ שָׁתוּל עַל מַיִם, וְעַל יוּבַל יְשַׁלַּח שָׁרָשָׁיו. וְלֹא יִרְאֶה כִּי יָבֹא חֹם, וְהָיָה עָלֵהוּ רַעֲנָן. וּבִשְׁנַת בַּצֹּרֶת לֹא יִדְאָג; וְלֹא יָמִישׁ מֵעֲשׂוֹת פֶּרִי."

[כג] רַבִּי אֶלְעָזָר בֶּן חִסְמָא אוֹמֵר: קִנִּין וּפִתְחֵי נִדָּה הֵן הֵן גּוּפֵי הֲלָכוֹת. תְּקוּפוֹת וְגִמַטְרִיָאוֹת פַּרְפְּרָאוֹת לַחָכְמָה.

---

21. דֶּרֶךְ אֶרֶץ . . . תּוֹרָה — **Torah . . . job.**
This was discussed in chapter 2, *mishnah* 2.

דַּעַת . . . בִּינָה — **Knowledge . . . understanding.**
Having דַּעַת, knowledge, means knowing how and why something works or happens. Having בִּינָה, understanding, means being able to understand one thing from another.

23. רַבִּי אֶלְעָזָר בֶּן חִסְמָא — **R' Elazar ben Chisma.**
This *Tanna* was one of the world's greatest mathematicians. Yet he taught that the main importance of astronomy and mathematics is using them as an aid to studying Torah law. The laws about קִנִּין, and נִדָּה are often very complicated and require a good knowledge of arithmetic. Ignorant people may think that these matters are not important Torah laws, but just examples for math experts. Or, if these foolish people see the rabbis working out the numbers, they may think that mathematics is more important than Torah study. To prevent these mistakes, R' Elazar tells us which study is only an introduction, and which is truly important.

1. **B**en Zoma taught: (a) Who is really wise? A person who learns from all people — as it is written in *Tehillim* (119:99), "From all who would teach me I grew wiser."

(b) Who is really strong? A person who overpowers his *yetzer hara* — as it is written in *Mishlei* (16:32), "It is better to be a person who does not get angry easily than to be a strong man; and it is better to be a person who controls his spirit than to be a conqueror of cities."

(c) Who is really rich? A person who is happy with whatever he has — as it is written in *Tehillim* (128:2), "If you work with your hands in order to earn what you need to eat, then you deserve praise and all is well with you." This means "you deserve praise" in this world, and "all is well with you" in the World to Come.

(d) Who really deserves honor? A person who honors other people — as the *Navi* (*Shmuel I* 2:30) writes, "*Hashem* said: Those people who honor Me, I will honor; but those people who treat Me disrespectfully will be cursed."

2. Ben Azzai taught: You should run to do a *mitzvah*, even if you think it is not important, and you should run away from a sin; for doing one *mitzvah* leads you to do another *mitzvah* and doing one sin leads you to do another sin; the reward for doing a *mitzvah* is the opportunity to do another *mitzvah* and the "reward" for doing a sin is the opportunity to do another sin.

[א] **בֶּן זוֹמָא** אוֹמֵר: אֵיזֶהוּ חָכָם? הַלּוֹמֵד מִכָּל אָדָם, שֶׁנֶּאֱמַר: "מִכָּל מְלַמְּדַי הִשְׂכַּלְתִּי."

אֵיזֶהוּ גִבּוֹר? הַכּוֹבֵשׁ אֶת יִצְרוֹ, שֶׁנֶּאֱמַר: "טוֹב אֶרֶךְ אַפַּיִם מִגִּבּוֹר, וּמֹשֵׁל בְּרוּחוֹ מִלֹּכֵד עִיר."

אֵיזֶהוּ עָשִׁיר? הַשָּׂמֵחַ בְּחֶלְקוֹ, שֶׁנֶּאֱמַר: "יְגִיעַ כַּפֶּיךָ כִּי תֹאכֵל אַשְׁרֶיךָ וְטוֹב לָךְ." "אַשְׁרֶיךָ" — בָּעוֹלָם הַזֶּה, "וְטוֹב לָךְ" — לָעוֹלָם הַבָּא.

אֵיזֶהוּ מְכֻבָּד? הַמְכַבֵּד אֶת הַבְּרִיּוֹת, שֶׁנֶּאֱמַר: "כִּי מְכַבְּדַי אֲכַבֵּד, וּבֹזַי יֵקַלּוּ."

[ב] בֶּן עַזַּאי אוֹמֵר: הֱוֵי רָץ לְמִצְוָה קַלָּה, וּבוֹרֵחַ מִן הָעֲבֵרָה; שֶׁמִּצְוָה גוֹרֶרֶת מִצְוָה, וַעֲבֵרָה גוֹרֶרֶת עֲבֵרָה, שֶׁשְּׂכַר מִצְוָה מִצְוָה, וּשְׂכַר עֲבֵרָה עֲבֵרָה.

אֵיזֶהוּ חָכָם ... גִּבּוֹר ... עָשִׁיר 1. — Who is really wise? ... strong? ... rich?

This does not mean that a person cannot be wise, strong or rich unless he acts exactly as this *mishnah* describes. It means that a person should not be proud of his wisdom, strength or riches unless he has earned them by following the lessons of the Torah — by learning from all people, controlling his temper, being happy with what he has, and honoring even people who are different from him. Such a person has the right to be proud of what he has accomplished.

יְגִיעַ כַּפֶּיךָ כִּי תֹאכֵל — If you work with your hands in order to earn what you need to eat.

Most people must work to support themselves and their families. Otherwise, they would have no food to eat and no clothing to wear. Many *mishnayos* in *Pirkei Avos* (for example 1:10, 2:2, and 3:21) teach us the importance of work. But a person should not make his work the most

important activity of his life. He should work enough to earn the things that are necessary. Once he has enough, he should spend most of his time doing *mitzvos* and studying Torah. That is what this sentence from *Tehillim* teaches: We should work with our hands in order to earn what we need, and then we should be happy with what we have.

כִּי מְכַבְּדַי אֲכַבֵּד — Those people who honor Me, I will honor.

We must show honor and respect to all people, even to those who may not deserve it. But there are certain people who really deserve honor. They are the ones who treat others with respect and honor.

We learn this from the way *Hashem* acts. *Hashem* is the King of the whole world. Everybody must honor Him. But He does not have to honor people. Still, *Hashem* does honor people who honor Him. Certainly, we must learn from *Hashem* and show respect and honor for those people who treat others with respect and honor.

Doing one mitzvah leads you to do another mitzvah.

3. He used to teach: You should never treat any person as if he is worthless, and you should never think that something is useless; because there is no person who does not have a time when he is needed, and there is no thing that does not have a place where it is needed.

4. R' Levitas of Yavneh taught:
You should be very,
very humble,
for a person's
measuring stick
should be
the worm.

[ג] הוּא הָיָה אוֹמֵר: אַל תְּהִי בָז לְכָל אָדָם, וְאַל תְּהִי מַפְלִיג לְכָל דָּבָר, שֶׁאֵין לְךָ אָדָם שֶׁאֵין לוֹ שָׁעָה, וְאֵין לְךָ דָּבָר שֶׁאֵין לוֹ מָקוֹם.

[ד] רַבִּי לְוִיטַס אִישׁ יַבְנֶה אוֹמֵר: מְאֹד מְאֹד הֱוֵי שְׁפַל רוּחַ, שֶׁתִּקְוַת אֱנוֹשׁ רִמָּה.

5. R' Yochanan ben Beroka taught: If any person disgraces God's Name, even in secret, Heaven will punish him in public. This is true whether he disgraced God's Name through carelessness or on purpose.

[ה] רַבִּי יוֹחָנָן בֶּן בְּרוֹקָא אוֹמֵר: כָּל הַמְּחַלֵּל שֵׁם שָׁמַיִם בַּסֵּתֶר, נִפְרָעִין מִמֶּנּוּ בְּגָלוּי. אֶחָד שׁוֹגֵג וְאֶחָד מֵזִיד בְּחִלּוּל הַשֵּׁם.

---

4. מְאֹד מְאֹד הֱוֵי שְׁפַל רוּחַ — You should be very, very humble.

The opposite of שְׁפַל רוּחַ, *humbleness*, is גַּאֲוָה, *arrogant pride*. In the case of other kinds of behavior, we learned that you should pick the in-between way. For example, don't be too stingy or too generous (see chapter 2, *mishnah* 1). This rule does not apply to humbleness and arrogance. When it comes to these two *middos*, you should be as humble as possible, because arrogance is the worst of all *middos*. Therefore, you should act so humble that you think of yourself as a tiny worm living under the earth.

But you must also remember that even worms have important jobs to do. That is what we learned in *mishnah* 3, "There is no thing that does not have a place where it is needed." Worms soften the earth so that the roots can spread out, and the rain water can reach them. Worms also help turn fallen leaves into rich earth that feeds the growing plants. We should learn from the worm that even though we have important work to do, we shouldn't make a lot of noise bragging about what we accomplish. The worm does not call out — as other animals seem to do — "Look at the wonderful things I am doing." It just goes about quietly doing what it should. And you must ask yourself, "Is this the way I act also?"

5. אֶחָד שׁוֹגֵג וְאֶחָד מֵזִיד בְּחִלּוּל הַשֵּׁם — This is true whether he disgraced God's Name through carelessness or on purpose.

A person who studies Torah should always treat other people nicely. He should be kind, gentle and friendly. Then people will say, "What a wonderful person! Look how nice a person who studies Torah acts. I wish my children would be like that." This creates a *kiddush Hashem*, it causes people to love *Hashem* and His Torah.

But if a person who studies Torah does not behave in a nice way, if he is fresh or loud or wild or just refuses to help other people, then people say, "Is this the way a Torah person acts? I don't want my children to be like that." This creates a *chillul Hashem*, it causes people to go away from the Torah and the *mitzvos*. It is a disgrace to God's Holy Name.

We must always remember that wherever we go and whatever we do, there are people who see us. And they judge us. Being kind and polite is a *kiddush Hashem*. Being fresh and unkind is a *chillul Hashem*. And it does not matter whether the politeness or freshness was on purpose or not, because the other person does not know what we were thinking. He only knows how we acted.

6. R' Yishmael bar R' Yose taught: If someone studies Torah in order to teach it to other people, Heaven will make certain that he will be able to learn and to teach. But if someone studies Torah in order to do the *mitzvos*, Heaven will make certain that he will be able to learn and to teach, to keep and to do the *mitzvos*.

7. R' Tzadok taught: (a) You should not separate yourself from everybody else. (b) If you are a judge, do not act as a lawyer. (c) You should not make the Torah into a crown to brag about, and you should not use it as a tool for earning your livelihood. This is what Hillel meant when he taught (chapter 1, *mishnah* 13), ''A person who uses his Torah knowledge selfishly will lose his reward.'' From this you learn that if someone uses the words of Torah for selfish benefits, in this world, that person removes himself from life in the World to Come.

8. R' Yose taught:

Whoever honors the Torah will himself be honored by people. Whoever disgraces the Torah will himself be disgraced by people.

9. R' Yishmael his son taught:

A person who avoids getting involved with court cases removes from himself hatred,

[ו] רַבִּי יִשְׁמָעֵאל בַּר רַבִּי יוֹסֵי אוֹמֵר: הַלּוֹמֵד עַל מְנָת לְלַמֵּד, מַסְפִּיקִין בְּיָדוֹ לִלְמוֹד וּלְלַמֵּד; וְהַלּוֹמֵד עַל מְנָת לַעֲשׂוֹת, מַסְפִּיקִין בְּיָדוֹ לִלְמוֹד וּלְלַמֵּד, לִשְׁמוֹר וְלַעֲשׂוֹת.

[ז] רַבִּי צָדוֹק אוֹמֵר: אַל תִּפְרוֹשׁ מִן הַצִּבּוּר; וְאַל תַּעַשׂ עַצְמְךָ כְּעוֹרְכֵי הַדַּיָּנִין; וְאַל תַּעֲשֶׂהָ עֲטָרָה לְהִתְגַּדֶּל בָּהּ, וְלֹא קַרְדֹּם לַחְפָּר בָּהּ. וְכָךְ הָיָה הִלֵּל אוֹמֵר: וְדִאשְׁתַּמֵּשׁ בְּתָגָא חֲלָף. הָא לָמַדְתָּ: כָּל הַנֶּהֱנֶה מִדִּבְרֵי תוֹרָה, נוֹטֵל חַיָּיו מִן הָעוֹלָם.

[ח] רַבִּי יוֹסֵי אוֹמֵר: כָּל הַמְּכַבֵּד אֶת הַתּוֹרָה, גּוּפוֹ מְכֻבָּד עַל הַבְּרִיּוֹת; וְכָל הַמְּחַלֵּל אֶת הַתּוֹרָה, גּוּפוֹ מְחֻלָּל עַל הַבְּרִיּוֹת.

[ט] רַבִּי יִשְׁמָעֵאל בְּנוֹ אוֹמֵר: הַחוֹשֵׂךְ עַצְמוֹ מִן הַדִּין, פּוֹרֵק מִמֶּנּוּ אֵיבָה

---

6. וְהַלּוֹמֵד עַל מְנָת לַעֲשׂוֹת — **But if someone studies Torah in order to do the mitzvos.**

Sometimes a person has bad *middos* and doesn't try to correct them, even though he knows he is doing the wrong thing. But he doesn't want his children to have bad *middos*, so he teaches them good *middos*. Then he says to them, ''Don't you do what I do. Just do as I say.'' That is not the proper way. You should study Torah to learn the *mitzvos* and good *middos* that the Torah teaches and to practice them. Then other people — especially your own children — will learn these *middos* and *mitzvos* from seeing how you behave.

7. אַל תִּפְרוֹשׁ . . . וְאַל תַּעַשׂ — **You should not separate yourself . . . do not act . . .**

These two lessons are taught in chapter 2 *mishnah* 5 and chapter 1, *mishnah* 8.

8. כָּל הַמְּכַבֵּד אֶת הַתּוֹרָה — **Whoever honors the Torah.**

This means many different things: honoring the *Sefer Torah*; respecting and honoring those who study and teach the Torah; and acting in a way that creates a *kiddush Hashem* (see *mishnah* 5).

וְכָל הַמְּחַלֵּל אֶת הַתּוֹרָה — **Whoever disgraces the Torah.**

This means dishonoring the *Sefer Torah* and those who study and teach Torah. It also means acting in a way that creates a *chillul Hashem*.

9. הַחוֹשֵׂךְ עַצְמוֹ מִן הַדִּין — **A person who avoids getting involved with court cases.**

An argument that is brought to *beis din* for a decision is called a *din Torah*. Some people are always ready to go to a *din Torah*. For example, whenever they disagree with their neighbor about their property, or with a storekeeper about something they bought, these people say, ''Let's go to a *din Torah*. We'll let the *beis din* decide.'' This is not a good *middah*, for three reasons:

(a) In court, the judge makes the final decision. Very often the loser will accuse the judge of taking a bribe and the witnesses of lying. He will then hate the judge, the witnesses and the winner. He will even think of them as his אֹיְבִים, *enemies*. That is why the *mishnah* calls this אֵיבָה, *hatred*.

(b) The judge may make a wrong decision and say that Reuvain must pay Shimon, when Shimon really should pay Reuvain. Then the wrong person ends up with the money, and it is considered like גֵּזֶל, *robbery*.

(c) The judge may ask one of the people to swear that he

robbery and false swearing. But if someone is too sure of himself in deciding the law, that person is foolish, wicked and arrogant.

10. He used to teach:

You should not be a judge all alone, for no one may judge by himself except *Hashem*, Who is One. After you have chosen two other people to be judges along with you, do not say to them, ''You must accept my opinion!'' For they who are the majority have the right to decide. But you by yourself may not.

11. R' Yonasan taught:

If any person studies the Torah and does its *mitzvos* even when he is poor, in the end he will study the Torah and do its *mitzvos* with riches. But if any person neglects the Torah because he is rich, in the end he will neglect the Torah because he will be poor.

וְגָזֵל וּשְׁבוּעַת שָׁוְא. וְהַגַּס לִבּוֹ בְּהוֹרָאָה, שׁוֹטֶה רָשָׁע וְגַס רוּחַ.

[י] הוּא הָיָה אוֹמֵר:

אַל תְּהִי דָן יְחִידִי, שֶׁאֵין דָּן יְחִידִי אֶלָּא אֶחָד. וְאַל תֹּאמַר: "קַבְּלוּ דַעְתִּי!" שֶׁהֵן רַשָּׁאִין וְלֹא אָתָּה.

[יא] רַבִּי יוֹנָתָן אוֹמֵר:

כָּל הַמְקַיֵּם אֶת הַתּוֹרָה מֵעָנִי, סוֹפוֹ לְקַיְּמָהּ מֵעְשֶׁר; וְכָל הַמְבַטֵּל אֶת הַתּוֹרָה מֵעְשֶׁר, סוֹפוֹ לְבַטְּלָהּ מֵעֹנִי.

---

is telling the truth. He may be wrong without knowing it. Then when he swears, it will be שְׁבוּעַת שָׁוְא, *false swearing*.

So when two people disagree, the best thing for them to do is to sit down and talk it over. Perhaps they will come to an agreement. And even if they don't, they should not run straight to *beis din*. Instead, they should ask a third person to help them settle their problem. If even that doesn't work, then they may go to *beis din*.

12. R' Meir taught:

(a) You should spend less time in your business so that you will have more time for studying Torah. (b) Be humble before every person. (c) If you wish to neglect the Torah, you will find many excuses to neglect it. But if you work hard at learning the Torah, *Hashem* has much reward to give you.

13. R' Eliezer ben Yaakov taught:

(a) A person who does even one *mitzvah* creates an angel who will take his side on the Day of Judgment. And a person who does even one sin creates an angel who will be against him on the Day of Judgment. (b) *Teshuvah* and good deeds are like a shield against punishment.

14. R' Yochanan the sandal maker taught:

Any gathering that is for the sake of Heaven will last forever. But if a gathering is not for the sake of Heaven, it will not last forever.

15. R' Elazar ben Shamua taught:

(a) Your student's honor should be as dear to you as your own. (b) Your friend's honor should be as important as your fear of your teacher. (c) And your fear of your teacher should be just as great as your fear of Heaven.

16. R' Yehudah taught:

You must be careful when you study, for if you make a wrong decision because you did not study carefully, it is considered as if you sinned on purpose.

[יב] רַבִּי מֵאִיר אוֹמֵר: הֱוֵי מְמַעֵט בְּעֵסֶק, וַעֲסֹק בַּתּוֹרָה, וֶהֱוֵי שְׁפַל רוּחַ בִּפְנֵי כָל אָדָם; וְאִם בָּטַלְתָּ מִן הַתּוֹרָה, יֶשׁ לָךְ בְּטֵלִים הַרְבֵּה כְּנֶגְדֶּךְ; וְאִם עָמַלְתָּ בַּתּוֹרָה, יֶשׁ לוֹ שָׂכָר הַרְבֵּה לִתֶּן לָךְ.

[יג] רַבִּי אֱלִיעֶזֶר בֶּן יַעֲקֹב אוֹמֵר: הָעוֹשֶׂה מִצְוָה אַחַת קוֹנֶה לוֹ פְּרַקְלִיט אֶחָד; וְהָעוֹבֵר עֲבֵרָה אַחַת, קוֹנֶה לוֹ קַטֵּיגוֹר אֶחָד. תְּשׁוּבָה וּמַעֲשִׂים טוֹבִים כִּתְרִיס בִּפְנֵי הַפֻּרְעָנוּת.

[יד] רַבִּי יוֹחָנָן הַסַּנְדְּלָר אוֹמֵר: כָּל כְּנֵסִיָּה שֶׁהִיא לְשֵׁם שָׁמַיִם, סוֹפָהּ לְהִתְקַיֵּם; וְשֶׁאֵינָהּ לְשֵׁם שָׁמַיִם, אֵין סוֹפָהּ לְהִתְקַיֵּם.

[טו] רַבִּי אֶלְעָזָר בֶּן שַׁמּוּעַ אוֹמֵר: יְהִי כְּבוֹד תַּלְמִידְךָ חָבִיב עָלֶיךָ כְּשֶׁלָּךְ; וּכְבוֹד חֲבֵרְךָ כְּמוֹרָא רַבָּךְ; וּמוֹרָא רַבָּךְ כְּמוֹרָא שָׁמַיִם.

[טז] רַבִּי יְהוּדָה אוֹמֵר: הֱוֵי זָהִיר בְּתַלְמוּד, שֶׁשִּׁגְגַת תַּלְמוּד עוֹלָה זָדוֹן.

---

14. רַבִּי יוֹחָנָן הַסַּנְדְּלָר — R' Yochanan the sandal maker.
Torah study must be combined with a way of earning a livelihood to support one's family (see chapter 2, *mishnah* 2). The *Tannaim* did not want to accept payment for teaching Torah. Each of them had a business or a profession or some other way of providing for his family's needs. Some of them were rich, some were poor. Some owned large properties, some worked at hard jobs. R' Yochanan made sandals; Hillel chopped wood; R' Yitzchak was a blacksmith. But all of them became great Torah scholars because they followed R' Meir's lesson (*mishnah* 12), "You should spend less time in your business so that you will have more time for studying Torah."

15. כְּבוֹד תַּלְמִידְךָ . . . וּכְבוֹד חֲבֵרְךָ . . . וּמוֹרָא רַבָּךְ — Your student's honor . . . Your friend's honor . . . And your fear of your teacher.

These three lessons can be learned from Moshe Rabbeinu, Aharon the *Kohein* and Yehoshua.

(a) Moshe *Rabbeinu* honored his student Yehoshua by treating him as an equal. Moshe said to him (*Shemos* 17:9), "We shall choose men for **our** army." He did not say, "I shall choose men for **my** army."

(b) Aharon the *Kohein* was Moshe *Rabbeinu*'s older brother, yet he honored Moshe as if he were his teacher. When Aharon had something to ask Moshe, he would say (*Bamidbar* 12:11), "Please, my master."

(c) When Yehoshua heard that two people had insulted his teacher Moshe, he said (*Bamidbar* 11:28), "My master Moshe, let them be destroyed," for he considered their disrespect for Moshe as disrespect for Hashem.

Your student's honor should be as dear to you as your own.

17. R' Shimon taught:

There are three crowns: The crown of the Torah; the crown of the *Kohein*; and the crown of the King. But the crown of a good name must be upon each of them.

[יז] רַבִּי שִׁמְעוֹן אוֹמֵר: שְׁלֹשָׁה כְתָרִים הֵם: כֶּתֶר תּוֹרָה, וְכֶתֶר כְּהֻנָּה, וְכֶתֶר מַלְכוּת; וְכֶתֶר שֵׁם טוֹב עוֹלֶה עַל גַּבֵּיהֶן.

18. R' Nehorai taught:

Leave your hometown to settle in a place of Torah, and do not think that the Torah will come looking for you. Only your study partners will make the Torah remain with you. As Shlomo *Hamelech* taught (*Mishlei* 3:5), "And you cannot depend only on your own understanding."

[יח] רַבִּי נְהוֹרַאי אוֹמֵר: הֱוֵי גוֹלֶה לִמְקוֹם תּוֹרָה, וְאַל תּאמַר שֶׁהִיא תָבוֹא אַחֲרֶיךָ, שֶׁחֲבֵרֶיךָ יְקַיְּמוּהָ בְיָדֶךָ. וְאֶל בִּינָתְךָ אַל תִּשָּׁעֵן.

19. R' Yannai taught:

We are not able to understand why some wicked people have an easy life or why some *tzaddikim* suffer.

[יט] רַבִּי יַנַּאי אוֹמֵר: אֵין בְּיָדֵינוּ לֹא מִשַּׁלְוַת הָרְשָׁעִים וְאַף לֹא מִיִּסּוּרֵי הַצַּדִּיקִים.

---

17. וְכֶתֶר שֵׁם טוֹב עוֹלֶה עַל גַּבֵּיהֶן — But the crown of a good name must be upon each of them.

A person should not wear a crown unless he deserves to. Even if someone has studied much Torah and is a great scholar, even if a *Kohein* has been appointed as *Kohein Gadol*, even if a prince has taken his father's place as the king, if any of them does not perform good deeds or is not well liked by other people, then he does not deserve to wear a crown.

But when a Torah scholar is known for his humility as Moshe *Rabbeinu* was (see *Bamidbar* 12:3), when a *Kohein* is famous for his kindness and love as Aharon was (see chapter 2, *mishnah* 12), or when a king is so well liked that he is nicknamed יְדִידְיָה, *God's beloved* (*Shmuel II* 12:25), as Shlomo *Hamelech* was, then he deserves to wear his crown.

19. אֵין בְּיָדֵינוּ — We are not able to understand.

Hashem's ways are hidden from us. Often we cannot explain why certain things happen. But we must remember that *Hashem* has His reasons, and they are always right. We cannot understand why *Hashem* does things because we can see only what is in front of us right now. But *Hashem* can see everything that is happening in the whole world and everything that ever happened at any time.

R' Yehoshua ibn Shuiv tells us a story from the *Midrash* that will help us to understand.

Moshe *Rabbeinu* once asked *Hashem* why a *tzaddik* sometimes suffers while an evil person lives in comfort.

Hashem replied by showing Moshe the following event:

A soldier lost his money pouch near a stream. Soon a poor boy came by, picked up the pouch, joyfully stuffed it under his shirt, and left for home.

A tired man then came to the stream, took a drink and lay back to rest. Soon he was fast asleep.

When the soldier discovered his money was missing, he rode back to the stream. He ran over to the sleeping man and shook him awake. "Where is my pouch? Give me back my money that you found!" he yelled.

"I don't know what you are talking about! I stopped to have a drink and then fell asleep. I found no money," said the man.

The soldier did not believe him. "Give me back my money or I will kill you."

"But I did not find any money," the man repeated. This made the soldier angry. He killed the man and searched through his belongings, but he did not find the money pouch.

Moshe *Rabbeinu* saw all this and said, "An innocent man was murdered. The murderer was not punished. And a poor boy became rich. *Hashem*, what does all this mean?"

20. R' Masya ben Charash taught:

(a) You should be the first to greet every person. (b) It is better to be the lions' tail than to be the foxes' head.

21. R' Yaakov taught:

This world is like a foyer before the World to Come. You must prepare yourself in the foyer so that you will be able to enter the banquet room.

22. He used to teach:

One hour of *teshuvah* and good deeds in this world is better than all of life in the World to Come. But one hour of spiritual pleasure in the World to Come is better than all of this world.

[כ] רַבִּי מַתְיָא בֶּן חָרָשׁ אוֹמֵר: הֱוֵי מַקְדִּים בִּשְׁלוֹם כָּל אָדָם, וֶהֱוֵי זָנָב לָאֲרָיוֹת, וְאַל תְּהִי רֹאשׁ לְשׁוּעָלִים.

[כא] רַבִּי יַעֲקֹב אוֹמֵר: הָעוֹלָם הַזֶּה דּוֹמֶה לִפְרוֹזְדוֹר בִּפְנֵי הָעוֹלָם הַבָּא, הַתְקֵן עַצְמְךָ בַּפְּרוֹזְדוֹר, כְּדֵי שֶׁתִּכָּנֵס לַטְּרַקְלִין.

[כב] הוּא הָיָה אוֹמֵר: יָפָה שָׁעָה אַחַת בִּתְשׁוּבָה וּמַעֲשִׂים טוֹבִים בָּעוֹלָם הַזֶּה מִכֹּל חַיֵּי הָעוֹלָם הַבָּא; וְיָפָה שָׁעָה אַחַת שֶׁל קוֹרַת רוּחַ בָּעוֹלָם הַבָּא מִכֹּל חַיֵּי הָעוֹלָם הַזֶּה.

Hashem answered by showing Moshe another event:

A man killed a farmer and stole his money. A soldier stood nearby watching, but did not move to help the farmer.

Then *Hashem* explained. "You may think that these two events have nothing to do with each other. But they do. I did not show you the two events in the order that they took place. You see, the soldier at the stream is the same soldier who stood by and did not help the farmer. When the farmer's murderer fled, he dropped the money pouch and the soldier picked it up. Later, as you saw, he lost it. The young boy who found it is the farmer's son, so the money is really his! And the man killed at the stream is the one who murdered and robbed the farmer.

"So now you know, Moshe, that the murderer was killed by the soldier who was a witness to his crime. And the money stolen from the farmer was returned to his son."

"Indeed," said Moshe, "all of *Hashem*'s ways are just."

20. זָנָב לַאֲרָיוֹת . . . רֹאשׁ לְשׁוּעָלִים — **Lions' tail . . . foxes' head.**

The foxes represent bad people — as Shlomo *Hamelech* described (*Shir Hashirim* 2:15), "The small foxes that destroy vineyards." If you are invited to join a club with members who do not follow the Torah and *mitzvos,* you should not accept the invitation. Even if they offer to make you their president or leader, you should not join them. The members of that club are like "foxes that destroy vineyards." Instead, you should remain with the "mighty lions" who are loyal to the Torah, even as just another member of the club and not an officer.

But if the people are willing to learn Torah and do the *mitzvos*, he may accept the job.

21-22. הָעוֹלָם הַזֶּה . . . הָעוֹלָם הַבָּא — **This world . . . the World to Come.**

There are three main stages in life. The first prepares us for the second, and the second prepares us for the third. The first stage prepares our bodies, and the second prepares our *neshamah*, or soul. The first stage takes place before a baby is born. The second stage begins with birth and ends when death releases the *neshamah* from its body. The third stage starts when the *neshamah* returns to Heaven.

The first stage lasts for nine months. During that time, all the parts of a baby's body develop: arms and legs, heart and stomach, eyes and ears. If, *chas veshalom*, a baby's body does not develop during this stage of its life, it will remain undeveloped all its life. People cannot grow fingers or ears or lungs after they are born.

Just as your body developed before you were born, your *neshamah* is developing while you are alive. You were born without responsibilities. But as you grow in size and intelligence, you learn to do more and more. As you grow older and wiser, you study Torah and learn which *middos* are good and which are not. You learn to do *mitzvos* and to avoid *aveiros*. When you do these *mitzvos*, when you study the Torah, when you act properly to other people and to *Hashem*, then your *neshamah* develops and becomes strong and healthy. This second stage is called *Olam Hazeh*, or this world. It is compared to a foyer because that is where the guests arrive before they enter the main banquet room.

The third stage is *Olam Haba*, the World to Come. It is the time for rewards. In *Olam Haba* you will receive the reward for the *mitzvos* you do, for the kindness you show, and for the Torah you learn in *Olam Hazeh*. The rewards of *Olam Haba* are greater, far far greater, than the best things in *Olam Hazeh*. One hour of pleasure that your *neshamah* will feel in *Olam Haba* is greater than all the pleasures of *Olam Hazeh*. That is why *Olam Haba* is called a banquet room. But in order to get these wonderful rewards, you must prepare yourself in *Olam Hazeh*. You can study more Torah and do more *mitzvos* in one hour in *Olam Hazeh* than you can do during all of *Olam Haba*.

Even at a very young age, you must prepare your *neshamah* in the foyer of *Olam Hazeh*; then you will be able to enter into, and receive the rewards of the banquet hall of *Olam Haba*.

23. R' Shimon ben Elazar taught: (a) You should not apologize to someone while his anger is still burning. (b) You should not try to ease someone's sadness while his dead relative is still before him. (c) You should not question someone about a promise that he just made. (d) And you should not try to see someone while he is in disgrace.

[כג] רַבִּי שִׁמְעוֹן בֶּן אֶלְעָזָר אוֹמֵר: אַל תְּרַצֶּה אֶת חֲבֵרְךָ בִּשְׁעַת כַּעֲסוֹ; וְאַל תְּנַחֲמֵהוּ בְּשָׁעָה שֶׁמֵּתוֹ מֻטָּל לְפָנָיו; וְאַל תִּשְׁאַל לוֹ בִּשְׁעַת נִדְרוֹ; וְאַל תִּשְׁתַּדֵּל לִרְאוֹתוֹ בִּשְׁעַת קַלְקָלָתוֹ.

23. אַל . . . בִּשְׁעַת — **Do not . . . while.**

Sometimes a *middah* takes hold of a person in a very strong way. For example, one may be very angry or very sad. At such times it is difficult for that person to think straight. It is hard to listen to an apology when full of anger. So if your mistake caused someone to become very angry (of course, you didn't do it on purpose), do not apologize while he is still angry and red in the face. Wait a while until he calms down, then make your apology.

Doing the right thing is important. Doing it at the proper time is even more important.

24. Shmuel *Hakattan* taught:

Always remember Shlomo *Hamelech's* lesson (*Mishlei* 24:17-18), ''You should not be happy when your enemy falls, and when he trips you should not let your heart fill with joy. Perhaps when *Hashem* sees you acting this way, He will consider you wicked and He may turn His anger from your enemy to you.''

25. Elisha ben Avuyah taught:

If someone studies Torah as a child, what is his learning like? It is like ink written on new paper. And if someone studies Torah in old age, what is his learning like? It is like ink written on smudged paper.

[כד] שְׁמוּאֵל הַקָּטָן אוֹמֵר:
"בִּנְפֹל אוֹיִבְךָ אַל תִּשְׂמָח, וּבִכָּשְׁלוֹ אַל יָגֵל לִבֶּךָ. פֶּן יִרְאֶה יהוה וְרַע בְּעֵינָיו, וְהֵשִׁיב מֵעָלָיו אַפּוֹ."

[כה] אֱלִישָׁע בֶּן אֲבוּיָה אוֹמֵר:
הַלּוֹמֵד יֶלֶד, לְמָה הוּא דוֹמֶה? לִדְיוֹ כְתוּבָה עַל נְיָר חָדָשׁ. וְהַלּוֹמֵד זָקֵן, לְמָה הוּא דוֹמֶה? לִדְיוֹ כְתוּבָה עַל נְיָר מָחוּק.

24. שְׁמוּאֵל הַקָּטָן — **Shmuel Hakattan.**

הַקָּטָן means ''the small one.'' Shmuel was called *Hakattan* because he was very humble. He would always make himself ''small.'' The Talmud (*Sanhedrin* 11a) tells a story that shows Shmuel *Hakattan's* humility:

One time, Rabban Gamliel asked the *Sanhedrin* to appoint seven Sages who would join him in declaring a leap year. The next morning eight Sages entered Rabban Gamliel's *beis din* room. Someone had decided to join the group without being invited. Rabban Gamliel said, ''The one who entered without permission should please leave.'' Hearing this, Shmuel *Hakattan* — who had been appointed — rose to his feet and said, ''I am the one who does not belong here. But still I would like to remain here, so that I may learn the *halachos* of how to declare a leap year.'' [Shmuel *Hakattan* did this because he did not want the guilty person to be

embarrassed.] Rabban Gamliel realized why Shmuel *Hakattan* said this, so he told him, ''Remain in your seat. You are certainly worthy of declaring a leap year.''

25. עַל נְיָר חָדָשׁ . . . נְיָר מָחוּק — **On new paper . . . smudged paper.**

This *mishnah* stresses the importance of learning Torah as a young child. However, it does not mean that an older person should not study Torah. A message written on smudged paper may not be as easy to read as one written on new paper, but it can be read. In the same way, a person who learns Torah when he is young, and continues learning Torah all of his life, will usually know more than a person who did not begin learning until late in life. But an older person can still gain much Torah knowledge and the rewards that it brings.

26. R' Yose bar Yehudah of Kfar Habavli taught:

If someone learns Torah from the young, what is he like? He is like a person who eats grapes that are not ripe and drinks wine that is not yet ready. But if someone learns Torah from older people, what is he like? He is like a person who eats ripe grapes and drinks aged wine.

[כו] רַבִּי יוֹסֵי בַּר יְהוּדָה אִישׁ כְּפַר הַבַּבְלִי אוֹמֵר: הַלוֹמֵד מִן הַקְּטַנִּים, לְמָה הוּא דוֹמֶה? לְאוֹכֵל עֲנָבִים קֵהוֹת, וְשׁוֹתֶה יַיִן מִגִּתּוֹ. וְהַלוֹמֵד מִן הַזְּקֵנִים, לְמָה הוּא דוֹמֶה? לְאוֹכֵל עֲנָבִים בְּשׁוּלוֹת, וְשׁוֹתֶה יַיִן יָשָׁן.

27. R' Meir taught:

You should not look at the barrel but at the wine that is in it. A new barrel may be filled with old wine, and an old barrel may not have any wine in it at all.

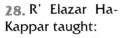

28. R' Elazar Ha-Kappar taught:

There are three bad things that remove a person from this world: Jealousy, desire and looking for honor.

29. He used to teach:

Those who were born will die. Those who have died will be brought back to life. Those who are alive will be judged. All this is that others should teach them, they should teach others, and they should teach themselves that He is God, He is the Maker, He is the Creator, He is the Understanding One, He is the Judge, He is the Witness, He is the Summoner. He is going to judge — Blessed is He — and with Him there is no wrongdoing, no forgetting, no playing favorites, and no taking bribes, for everything belongs to Him.

And you should know that everything is done according to the account of what you did. So do not let your *yetzer hara* promise you that you will not be punished after you die. For just as you could not prevent yourself from being created, and you could not prevent yourself from being born, and you could not prevent yourself from living, and you could not prevent yourself from dying — in the same way you cannot prevent yourself from having to explain all of your actions before *Hashem*, the King of kings, the Holy One, Blessed is He.

[כז] רַבִּי מֵאִיר אוֹמֵר: אַל תִּסְתַּכֵּל בַּקַּנְקַן, אֶלָּא בְּמַה שֶׁיֵּשׁ בּוֹ; יֵשׁ קַנְקַן חָדָשׁ מָלֵא יָשָׁן, וְיָשָׁן שֶׁאֲפִילוּ חָדָשׁ אֵין בּוֹ.

[כח] רַבִּי אֶלְעָזָר הַקַּפָּר אוֹמֵר: הַקִּנְאָה וְהַתַּאֲוָה וְהַכָּבוֹד מוֹצִיאִין אֶת הָאָדָם מִן הָעוֹלָם.

[כט] הוּא הָיָה אוֹמֵר: הַיְלוֹדִים לָמוּת, וְהַמֵּתִים לִחְיוֹת, וְהַחַיִּים לִדּוֹן — לֵידַע לְהוֹדִיעַ וּלְהִוָּדַע שֶׁהוּא אֵל, הוּא הַיּוֹצֵר, הוּא הַבּוֹרֵא, הוּא הַמֵּבִין, הוּא הַדַּיָּן, הוּא הָעֵד, הוּא בַּעַל דִּין, הוּא עָתִיד לָדוֹן. בָּרוּךְ הוּא, שֶׁאֵין לְפָנָיו לֹא עַוְלָה, וְלֹא שִׁכְחָה, וְלֹא מַשֹּׂא פָנִים, וְלֹא מִקַּח שֹׁחַד; שֶׁהַכֹּל שֶׁלּוֹ. וְדַע, שֶׁהַכֹּל לְפִי הַחֶשְׁבּוֹן. וְאַל יַבְטִיחֲךָ יִצְרְךָ שֶׁהַשְּׁאוֹל בֵּית מָנוֹס לָךְ — שֶׁעַל כָּרְחֲךָ אַתָּה נוֹצָר; וְעַל כָּרְחֲךָ אַתָּה נוֹלָד; וְעַל כָּרְחֲךָ אַתָּה חַי; וְעַל כָּרְחֲךָ אַתָּה מֵת; וְעַל כָּרְחֲךָ אַתָּה עָתִיד לִתֵּן דִּין וְחֶשְׁבּוֹן לִפְנֵי מֶלֶךְ מַלְכֵי הַמְּלָכִים, הַקָּדוֹשׁ בָּרוּךְ הוּא.

---

27. אַל תִּסְתַּכֵּל בַּקַּנְקַן אֶלָּא בְּמַה שֶׁיֵּשׁ בּוֹ — **You should not look at the barrel but at the wine that is in it.**

The Torah is compared to wine. Most wines get better with age. If wine stands in a wooden barrel for many years it gains a special flavor. As time passes the wine develops a delicious taste. New wine does not have this flavor and taste. In the same way, when Torah is studied over a long period of time, it develops a depth and a scope that short-term learning does not have.

Just as wine represents Torah, barrels represent people. We would expect old barrels to hold old wine and new barrels to hold new wine; old people to have learned much Torah and young people to have learned little. However, this is not always true. Sometimes a new barrel (a youngster) may be full of old wine (Torah wisdom), while an old barrel (an elderly person) is empty.

This is also the meaning of the expression, "Never judge a book by its cover."

1. **H**ashem created the world with ten commands. And what does this teach us? He certainly could have created the world with only one command! He created

[א] בַּעֲשָׂרָה מַאֲמָרוֹת נִבְרָא הָעוֹלָם. וּמַה תַּלְמוּד לוֹמַר? וַהֲלֹא בְּמַאֲמָר אֶחָד יָכוֹל לְהִבָּרְאוֹת?

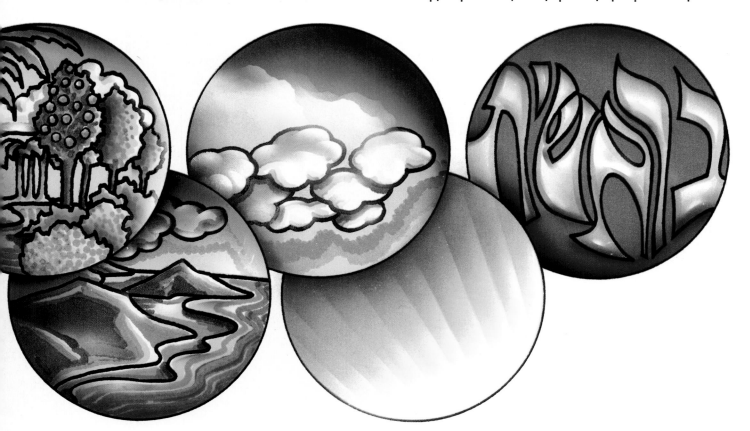

1. בַּעֲשָׂרָה — With ten.

The first eight *mishnayos* of this chapter do not seem to belong in *Avos*. Instead of teaching *middos*, they speak about history: the Creation; The first twenty generations of mankind; Avraham *Avinu*; the Jews in Egypt, at the sea, and in the desert; the *Beis Hamikdash*. Why are these *mishnayos* included here?

To answer this question we must first answer another question. How do we know which *middos* are good and which are bad? One way we can tell this is by studying the *middos* of *Hashem*. You can be sure that if *Hashem* acts in a certain way, that must be a good *middah* for us to learn. As the Talmud (*Sotah* 14a) teaches us, "Just as He gives clothing to those who need them, so should you give clothing to those who need them. Just as He visits the sick, so should you visit the sick."

Many of these *middos* can be learned from these eight *mishnayos*. They teach us how much God loves the world He created, and how Avraham *Avinu* returned that love.

They tell how carefully *Hashem* planned everything He did; how He showed his special love for the Jewish people; how slow He is to anger. These are all lessons in *middos* for us to follow.

בַּעֲשָׂרָה מַאֲמָרוֹת נִבְרָא הָעוֹלָם — Hashem created the world with ten commands.

The Torah uses the expression וַיֹּאמֶר אֱלֹקִים, *God said*, nine times in the story of Creation. Each of these sayings was a command for something new to come into being: light; sky; sea and land; plants; sun, moon and stars; fish and birds; land animals; people; and the ability of plants to nourish people and animals. But even before the first וַיֹּאמֶר, the Torah speaks of the heavens and the earth. These were also created by a command from God — as it is written in *Tehillim* (33:6), "בִּדְבַר ה' שָׁמַיִם נַעֲשׂוּ, The heavens were made by *Hashem's* word." The *Gemara* (*Rosh Hashanah* 32a) tells us that this command was the word בְּרֵאשִׁית, the first word in the Torah. So all together, God used ten commands to create the world.

the world with ten commands in order to punish the wicked people who destroy the world that was created with ten commands; and to give a good reward to the *tzaddikim* who keep up the world that was created with ten commands.

אֶלָּא לְהִפָּרַע מִן הָרְשָׁעִים, שֶׁמְּאַבְּדִין אֶת הָעוֹלָם שֶׁנִּבְרָא בַּעֲשָׂרָה מַאֲמָרוֹת, וְלִתֵּן שָׂכָר טוֹב לַצַּדִּיקִים, שֶׁמְּקַיְּמִין אֶת הָעוֹלָם שֶׁנִּבְרָא בַּעֲשָׂרָה מַאֲמָרוֹת.

וַהֲלֹא בְמַאֲמָר אֶחָד יָכוֹל לְהִבָּרְאוֹת — He certainly could have created the world with only one command!

When we love what we are doing, we don't care how long it takes us. In fact, we sometimes take extra steps and more time than we really need to finish the job. For example, it is easy to buy a birthday card for your brother or sister. Making your own card is harder and takes a lot more time. But it also shows that you care enough to put in that extra effort. This is also true about doing *mitzvos*. Anybody can buy delicious *challos* in the local bakery. But many women want to show an extra special love for *Shabbos*. And so they take the time to bake their own *challos*.

In the same way, when God created the world, He wanted us to know how much He loves the world and everything in it. So even though He could have made the whole world by saying, "Let the world come into being," He didn't do that. Instead, He took six days and spoke ten commands to create the world.

Now let us return to the example of the birthday card.

Make believe you bought your brother a beautiful card. Then, when you gave it to him, he said, "Oh! What an ugly card!" and tore it up. That would make you feel bad. But you would feel much worse if he did that to a card you made yourself, one that took a long time and a lot of work. And let us imagine that the opposite happened. When you gave him the store-bought card, he liked it and said, "Thank you for remembering my birthday and for this beautiful card!" That would make you feel good. But what if you gave him a homemade card and he said, "Oh! What a beautiful card! I must save it and show it to everyone!" Then you would feel really great.

In the same way, when a person sins, *Hashem* feels very sad (so to speak) and says, "Look how that person is destroying the world that I made with so much love. Now I will have to punish him for his wicked ways." But when a person does *mitzvos*, *Hashem* is happy and says, "Look how that person takes care of the world that I made with so much love. Now I will reward him for all the good things he has done."

2. There were ten generations from Adam to Noach — to show how slow *Hashem* is to anger; for all those generations did more and more things to make *Hashem* angry, until He brought the waters of the Flood upon them.

3. There were ten generations from Noach until Avraham — to show how slow *Hashem* is to anger; for all those generations did more and more things to make *Hashem* angry, until Avraham *Avinu* came and received the reward they would have received if they had been worthy.

4. Avraham *Avinu* was given ten tests, and he passed all of them. This shows how great was Avraham *Avinu's* love for *Hashem*.

5. *Hashem* performed ten miracles for our ancestors in Egypt and ten more miracles at the sea. The Holy One, Blessed is He, also brought ten plagues upon the Egyptians in Egypt and ten more plagues at the sea.

[ב] עֲשָׂרָה דוֹרוֹת מֵאָדָם וְעַד נֹחַ, לְהוֹדִיעַ כַּמָּה אֶרֶךְ אַפַּיִם לְפָנָיו; שֶׁכָּל הַדּוֹרוֹת הָיוּ מַכְעִיסִין וּבָאִין, עַד שֶׁהֵבִיא עֲלֵיהֶם אֶת מֵי הַמַּבּוּל.

[ג] עֲשָׂרָה דוֹרוֹת מִנֹּחַ וְעַד אַבְרָהָם, לְהוֹדִיעַ כַּמָּה אֶרֶךְ אַפַּיִם לְפָנָיו; שֶׁכָּל הַדּוֹרוֹת הָיוּ מַכְעִיסִין וּבָאִין, עַד שֶׁבָּא אַבְרָהָם אָבִינוּ וְקִבֵּל שְׂכַר כֻּלָּם.

[ד] עֲשָׂרָה נִסְיוֹנוֹת נִתְנַסָּה אַבְרָהָם אָבִינוּ וְעָמַד בְּכֻלָּם, לְהוֹדִיעַ כַּמָּה חִבָּתוֹ שֶׁל אַבְרָהָם אָבִינוּ.

[ה] עֲשָׂרָה נִסִּים נַעֲשׂוּ לַאֲבוֹתֵינוּ בְּמִצְרַיִם וַעֲשָׂרָה עַל הַיָּם. עֶשֶׂר מַכּוֹת הֵבִיא הַקָּדוֹשׁ בָּרוּךְ הוּא עַל הַמִּצְרִים בְּמִצְרַיִם וְעֶשֶׂר עַל הַיָּם.

2-3. נֹחַ . . . אַבְרָהָם — Noach . . . Avraham.

Noach was a *tzaddik*. He did not learn from the bad people of his times, but he did not teach them to be good either. That is why, when the whole world was destroyed by the Flood, Noach was able to save only himself and his family. Avraham *Avinu* was an even greater *tzaddik*. He did not learn from the bad people of his times. Instead, he taught them to be good but they didn't want to listen. That is why Avraham was given all the rewards that would have gone to the people who lived before him. If he had lived in those earlier years, he also would have taught the people of those times to follow the ways of *Hashem*.

4. עֲשָׂרָה נִסְיוֹנוֹת — Ten tests.

God tested Avraham *Avinu* ten times: (a) King Nimrod threw him into the fiery furnace (*Bereishis* 11:28, see *Rashi*); (b) God commanded him to leave his home to travel to an unknown land (12:1); (c) when he got to that land, there was a hunger and he had to move again (12:10); (d) in Egypt, his wife Sarah was kidnapped by the king (12:15); (e) in order to save his nephew Lot, he had to fight the armies of four mighty kings (14:13-16); (f) he was told that his children would be slaves in a foreign land (15:13); (g) he was commanded to have a *bris milah* (17:9-14); (h) his wife Sarah was kidnapped by Avimelech, King of Gerar (20:2); (i) he was commanded to send away Hagar and Yishmael (21:10-12); (j) he was commanded to offer his son Yitzchak as a sacrifice (22:1-2).

5. עֲשָׂרָה נִסִּים . . . עֶשֶׂר מַכּוֹת — Ten miracles . . . ten plagues.

These are the same. Ten plagues attacked the Egyptians. The miracles were that they did not bother the Jews.

וַעֲשָׂרָה עַל הַיָּם — And ten more miracles at the Sea.

If we study all the places in *Tanach* where קְרִיעַת יַם סוּף, *the Splitting of the Sea,* is mentioned, we will find ten miracles. They are: (a) the waters split; (b) not only did they split, but they separated into twelve paths so that each of the twelve tribes had its own path; (c) in order that each tribe should know that the other tribes were safe, the walls of water that separated them became crystal clear; (d) the waters formed roofs over the Jews; (e) the muddy sea bottom turned dry, and (f) formed itself into a brick road as the Jews crossed, but (g) turned muddy for the Egyptians who chased them; (h) the walls between the paths were frozen solid and were as hard as rock, yet (i) fountains of sweet water spurted from these walls, so that the Jews were able to drink; and (j) the water they did not drink froze into beautiful shapes.

וְעֶשֶׂר עַל הַיָּם — And ten more plagues at the sea.

In אָז יָשִׁיר, *the Song at the Sea,* that the Jews sang to thank *Hashem* for saving them from the Egyptians (*Shemos* 15:1-9), there are ten words that describe how the Egyptians drowned. Each word has a slightly different meaning. So we see that they drowned in ten different ways.

The Holy One, Blessed is He, brought
ten plagues upon the Egyptians in Egypt.

6. Our ancestors tested the Holy One, Blessed is He, with ten tests in the desert — as it is written (*Bamidbar* 14:22), ''*Hashem* said: They tested Me these ten times, and they did not listen to My voice.''

7. Ten miracles were done for our ancestors in the *Beis Hamikdash:* (a) No pregnant woman every lost her baby because of the smell of the burning meat of the *korbanos.* (b) The meat of the *korbanos* never became spoiled. (c) No fly was ever seen in the place where the meat of the *korbanos* was butchered. (d) The *Kohein Gadol* never had a *tumah* accident on Yom Kippur. (e) The rain never put out the fire on top of the *mizbe'ach.* (f) The wind never upset the column of smoke that rose straight up from the *mizbe'ach.* (g) The *Omer,* the Two Breads, and the *Lechem Hapanim* never became invalid. (h) The crowds were so great that the people stood pressed closely together, yet there was plenty of room for them all to bow at the same time. (i) Snakes and scorpions never harmed anyone in *Yerushalayim.* (j) And no man every said to his friend, ''There is not enough room for me to stay overnight in *Yerusha-layim.*''

8. Ten things were created just before *Shabbos* during the Six Days of Creation, and they are: (a) The mouth of the earth; (b) the mouth of the well; (c) the mouth of the donkey; (d) the rainbow; (e) the *mann;* (f) the stick; (g) the *shamir* worm; (h) the letters; (i) the writing; and (j) the *Luchos.* Some of the Sages add the destructive spirits; Moshe *Rabbeinu's* grave; and Avraham *Avinu's* ram. Some add the tongs with which the first tongs were made.

[ו] עֲשָׂרָה נִסְיוֹנוֹת נִסּוּ אֲבוֹתֵינוּ אֶת הַקָּדוֹשׁ בָּרוּךְ הוּא בַּמִּדְבָּר, שֶׁנֶּאֱמַר: "וַיְנַסּוּ אֹתִי זֶה עֶשֶׂר פְּעָמִים, וְלֹא שָׁמְעוּ בְּקוֹלִי.''

[ז] עֲשָׂרָה נִסִּים נַעֲשׂוּ לַאֲבוֹתֵינוּ בְּבֵית הַמִּקְדָּשׁ: לֹא הִפִּילָה אִשָּׁה מֵרֵיחַ בְּשַׂר הַקֹּדֶשׁ; וְלֹא הִסְרִיחַ בְּשַׂר הַקֹּדֶשׁ מֵעוֹלָם; וְלֹא נִרְאָה זְבוּב בְּבֵית הַמִּטְבָּחַיִם; וְלֹא אֵירַע קֶרִי לְכֹהֵן גָּדוֹל בְּיוֹם הַכִּפּוּרִים; וְלֹא כִבּוּ הַגְּשָׁמִים אֵשׁ שֶׁל עֲצֵי הַמַּעֲרָכָה; וְלֹא נִצְּחָה הָרוּחַ אֶת עַמּוּד הֶעָשָׁן; וְלֹא נִמְצָא פְסוּל בָּעֹמֶר, וּבִשְׁתֵּי הַלֶּחֶם, וּבְלֶחֶם הַפָּנִים; עוֹמְדִים צְפוּפִים, וּמִשְׁתַּחֲוִים רְוָחִים; וְלֹא הִזִּיק נָחָשׁ וְעַקְרָב בִּירוּשָׁלַיִם מֵעוֹלָם; וְלֹא אָמַר אָדָם לַחֲבֵרוֹ: "צַר לִי הַמָּקוֹם שֶׁאָלִין בִּירוּשָׁלָיִם.''

[ח] עֲשָׂרָה דְבָרִים נִבְרְאוּ בְּעֶרֶב שַׁבָּת בֵּין הַשְּׁמָשׁוֹת, וְאֵלוּ הֵן; פִּי הָאָרֶץ, וּפִי הַבְּאֵר, פִּי הָאָתוֹן, וְהַקֶּשֶׁת, וְהַמָּן, וְהַמַּטֶּה, וְהַשָּׁמִיר, הַכְּתָב, וְהַמִּכְתָּב, וְהַלּוּחוֹת. וְיֵשׁ אוֹמְרִים: אַף הַמַּזִּיקִין, וּקְבוּרָתוֹ שֶׁל מֹשֶׁה, וְאֵילוֹ שֶׁל אַבְרָהָם אָבִינוּ. וְיֵשׁ אוֹמְרִים: אַף צְבָת בִּצְבָת עֲשׂוּיָה.

---

6. עֲשָׂרָה נִסְיוֹנוֹת — **Ten tests.**
Whatever *Hashem* does is good. Even if we do not understand why He does something, we must always have אֱמוּנָה, *faith*, that it is good. Whenever someone complains about the way God treats him, it is as if he is testing *Hashem* to see if He is really doing something good. During the forty years that our ancestors were in the desert, they complained or disobeyed God's command ten times: (a) When the Egyptians chased them to the sea (*Shemos* 14:11); (b) when they had nothing to drink but the bitter waters of Marah (15:24); (c) when they ran out of food (16:3); (d) when they left over *mann,* even though they had been told not to (16:20); (e) when they left the camp to gather *mann* on *Shabbos* even though they had been told not to (16:27); (f) when their water ran out at Refidim (17:2); (g) when they worshiped the Golden Calf (32:4); (h) when they rebelled against *Hashem's* *mitzvos* (*Bamidbar* 11:1); (i) when they complained that the *mann* was not good (11:4); and (j) when they believed the spies' evil report about *Eretz Yisrael* (14:22).

8. These are the ten things that were created just before *Shabbos* during the Six Days of Creation: (a) the mouth of the earth, where Korach and his followers were swallowed up (*Bamidbar* 16:31-35); (b) the mouth of the well (*Bamidbar* 21:16-20); (c) the mouth of the donkey that spoke to Bilam (*Bamidbar* 22:28); (d) the rainbow that was shown to Noach as a sign that there would not be another world-wide flood (*Bereishis* 9:12-15); (e) the *mann;* (f) the stick that Moshe *Rabbeinu* used to do the miracles (*Shemos* 4:17); (g) the worm called *shamir,* which cut the stones for the *Beis Hamikdash* (*Sotah* 48b); (h) the letters of the *aleph-beis;* (i) the way in which *Hashem* wrote the Ten Commandments on the *Luchos,* so that they went all the way through the *Luchos* and could be read on all four sides; and (j) the *Luchos.*
Some of the Sages say that three more things were created at that time: the destructive spirits; Moshe *Rabbeinu's* grave; and the ram that Avraham *Avinu* offered in place of Yitzchak (*Bereishis* 22:13). Some of the Sages say that the first tongs were also created at this time, for people must have tongs to make tongs.

Ten things were created just before Shabbos during the Six Days of Creation.

9. There are seven *middos* of a stupid person and seven *middos* of a wise person. The *middos* of a wise person are: (a) He does not speak before someone who is wiser or older than he is; (b) he does not interrupt when someone else is speaking; (c) he does not answer questions in a hurry; (d) he asks proper questions and gives proper answers; (e) he discusses first things first and last things last; (f) if he is asked about something that he never heard, he says, "I have not heard about this"; and (g) he admits the truth when he realizes his mistake.

A stupid person does just the opposite.

10. Seven kinds of punishment come upon the world for seven kinds of sin: (a) If some people give *ma'aser* and some people do not, hunger comes, caused by a shortage of rain. Then some people go hungry and others eat their fill. (b) If everyone decides not to give *ma'aser*, then hunger comes, caused by attacking armies and shortage of rain. Then everyone goes hungry. (c) If they decide not to give *challah*, no rain falls. This causes a hunger, and everyone goes hungry.

11. (d) Deadly plagues come upon the world when people do sins that deserve the death penalty, but *beis din* was not given the right to punish them; and also when people buy and sell crops of a *shemittah* year. (e) The sword of war comes upon the world when judges delay carrying out justice or give unfair judgments, and when people explain the Torah in ways that are not like the *halachah*. (f) Wild beasts come upon the world as punishment for unnecessary swearing and for *chillul Hashem*. (g) Exile comes upon the world as punishment for idol worship, for immorality, for murder, and for working the earth during the *shemittah* year.

12. At four times during every seven-year *shemittah* period deadly plagues increase: (a) at the beginning of the fourth year; (b) at the beginning of the seventh year; (c) just after the seventh year has ended; and (d) every year right after Succos.

[ט] שִׁבְעָה דְבָרִים בַּגֹּלֶם, וְשִׁבְעָה בֶחָכָם. חָכָם אֵינוֹ מְדַבֵּר לִפְנֵי מִי שֶׁגָּדוֹל מִמֶּנּוּ בְּחָכְמָה וּבְמִנְיָן; וְאֵינוֹ נִכְנָס לְתוֹךְ דִּבְרֵי חֲבֵרוֹ; וְאֵינוֹ נִבְהָל לְהָשִׁיב; שׁוֹאֵל כְּעִנְיָן, וּמֵשִׁיב כַּהֲלָכָה; וְאוֹמֵר עַל רִאשׁוֹן רִאשׁוֹן, וְעַל אַחֲרוֹן אַחֲרוֹן; וְעַל מַה שֶּׁלֹּא שָׁמַע אוֹמֵר: "לֹא שָׁמַעְתִּי"; וּמוֹדֶה עַל הָאֱמֶת. וְחִלּוּפֵיהֶן בַּגֹּלֶם.

[י] שִׁבְעָה מִינֵי פֻּרְעָנִיּוֹת בָּאִין לָעוֹלָם עַל שִׁבְעָה גוּפֵי עֲבֵרָה: מִקְצָתָן מְעַשְּׂרִין וּמִקְצָתָן אֵינָן מְעַשְּׂרִין, רָעָב שֶׁל בַּצֹּרֶת בָּא, מִקְצָתָן רְעֵבִים וּמִקְצָתָן שְׂבֵעִים; גָּמְרוּ שֶׁלֹּא לְעַשֵּׂר, רָעָב שֶׁל מְהוּמָה וְשֶׁל בַּצֹּרֶת בָּא; וְשֶׁלֹּא לִטֹּל אֶת הַחַלָּה, רָעָב שֶׁל כְּלָיָה בָּא;

[יא] דֶּבֶר בָּא לָעוֹלָם – עַל מִיתוֹת הָאֲמוּרוֹת בַּתּוֹרָה שֶׁלֹּא נִמְסְרוּ לְבֵית דִּין, וְעַל פֵּרוֹת שְׁבִיעִית; חֶרֶב בָּאָה לָעוֹלָם – עַל עִנּוּי הַדִּין, וְעַל עִוּוּת הַדִּין, וְעַל הַמּוֹרִים בַּתּוֹרָה שֶׁלֹּא כַהֲלָכָה; חַיָּה רָעָה בָאָה לָעוֹלָם – עַל שְׁבוּעַת שָׁוְא, וְעַל חִלּוּל הַשֵּׁם; גָּלוּת בָּאָה לָעוֹלָם – עַל עוֹבְדֵי עֲבוֹדָה זָרָה, וְעַל גִּלּוּי עֲרָיוֹת, וְעַל שְׁפִיכוּת דָּמִים, וְעַל שְׁמִטַּת הָאָרֶץ.

[יב] בְּאַרְבָּעָה פְרָקִים הַדֶּבֶר מִתְרַבֶּה: בָּרְבִיעִית, וּבַשְּׁבִיעִית, וּבְמוֹצָאֵי שְׁבִיעִית, וּבְמוֹצָאֵי הֶחָג שֶׁבְּכָל שָׁנָה וְשָׁנָה.

11. וְעַל שְׁמִטַּת הָאָרֶץ — **And for working the earth during the shemittah year.**

Every seventh year is set aside as *shemittah*. During that year the land may not be plowed, nothing may be planted, and fruit may not be taken from the trees in the usual way. A farmer who obeys all the laws of *shemittah* shows that he considers *Hashem* to be the true owner of the land.

However, if a farmer does not obey these laws, he shows that he thinks of himself — not *Hashem* — as the real owner of the land. *Hashem* exiles such a person from the land, to teach him that he is not the true owner. Then he has a chance to do *teshuvah* for not following the *mitzvah* of *shemittah*.

(a) At the beginning of the fourth year, plagues come because people did not give the *ma'aser* that they were supposed to give to the poor during the third year; (b) at the beginning of the seventh, because people did not give the *ma'aser* that they were supposed to give to the poor during the sixth year; (c) just after the seventh year has ended, because people did not keep the *mitzvos* of *shemittah* fruit; and (d) every year right after *Succos*, because people robbed the poor of the gifts that the Torah assigned for them.

13. There are four ways people act about sharing their belongings: (a) If a person says, "Anything that belongs to me is only for my use; and anything that belongs to you is only for your use" — that person is in between, he is neither good nor bad. But some of the Sages say that this is the way the people of Sodom acted. (b) If a person says, "I will let you use anything that belongs to me, but only if you let me use anything that belongs to you" — he is a common person. (c) If a person says, "I will let you use anything that belongs to me, even though I will not use anything that belongs to you" — that person is a *chassid* who does more for other people than the *halachah* demands. (d) If a person says, "You must let me use anything that belongs to you, even though I do not let you use anything that belongs to me" — that person is wicked.

בָּרְבִיעִית, מִפְּנֵי מַעֲשַׂר עָנִי שֶׁבַּשְּׁלִישִׁית; בַּשְּׁבִיעִית, מִפְּנֵי מַעֲשַׂר עָנִי שֶׁבַּשִּׁשִׁית; בְּמוֹצָאֵי שְׁבִיעִית, מִפְּנֵי פֵּרוֹת שְׁבִיעִית; בְּמוֹצָאֵי הֶחָג שֶׁבְּכָל שָׁנָה וְשָׁנָה, מִפְּנֵי גֶּזֶל מַתְּנוֹת עֲנִיִּים.

[יג] אַרְבַּע מִדּוֹת בָּאָדָם. הָאוֹמֵר: "שֶׁלִּי שֶׁלִּי וְשֶׁלְּךָ שֶׁלָּךְ," זוֹ מִדָּה בֵּינוֹנִית, וְיֵשׁ אוֹמְרִים: זוֹ מִדַּת סְדוֹם; "שֶׁלִּי שֶׁלָּךְ וְשֶׁלְּךָ שֶׁלִּי," עַם הָאָרֶץ; "שֶׁלִּי שֶׁלָּךְ וְשֶׁלְּךָ שֶׁלָּךְ," חָסִיד; "שֶׁלְּךָ שֶׁלִּי וְשֶׁלִּי שֶׁלִּי," רָשָׁע.

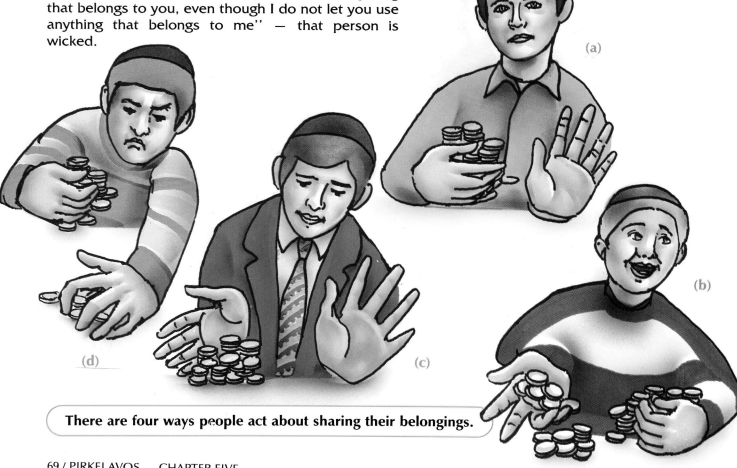

(a)

(b)

(c)

(d)

There are four ways people act about sharing their belongings.

14. There are four ways people act when something happens to make them angry: (a) If a person is very quick to anger, and is also very quick to calm down — he loses more for getting angry quickly and often than he gains for calming down quickly. (b) If a person is very slow to anger, and also very slow to calm down — he gains more for not getting angry quickly and often than he loses for not calming down quickly. (c) If a person is very slow to anger and very quick to calm down — that person is a *chassid* who is very careful how he acts towards other people. (d) If a person is very quick to anger and very slow to calm down — that person is wicked.

15. There are four kinds of students: (a) If a student understands quickly, but also forgets quickly — he loses more than he gains, because he has wasted his time. (b) If a student understands slowly and also forgets slowly — he gains more than he loses. (c) If a student understands quickly and forgets slowly — he has a good portion. (d) If a student understands slowly and forgets quickly — he has a bad portion.

16. There are four ways people act about giving charity: (a) If a person wants to give charity, but does not want other people to give — he sees others in a bad way. (b) If a person wants other people to give charity, but does not want to give himself — he sees himself in a bad way. (c) If a person wants to give charity, and also wants other people to give — he is a *chassid*. (d) If a person does not want to give charity, and also does not want others to give — he is wicked.

[יד] אַרְבַּע מִדּוֹת בַּדֵּעוֹת: נֽוֹחַ לִכְעוֹס וְנֽוֹחַ לִרְצוֹת, יָצָא שְׂכָרוֹ בְּהֶפְסֵדוֹ; קָשֶׁה לִכְעוֹס וְקָשֶׁה לִרְצוֹת, יָצָא הֶפְסֵדוֹ בִּשְׂכָרוֹ; קָשֶׁה לִכְעוֹס וְנֽוֹחַ לִרְצוֹת, חָסִיד; נֽוֹחַ לִכְעוֹס וְקָשֶׁה לִרְצוֹת, רָשָׁע.

[טו] אַרְבַּע מִדּוֹת בַּתַּלְמִידִים: מָהִיר לִשְׁמֽוֹעַ וּמָהִיר לְאַבֵּד, יָצָא שְׂכָרוֹ בְּהֶפְסֵדוֹ; קָשֶׁה לִשְׁמֽוֹעַ וְקָשֶׁה לְאַבֵּד, יָצָא הֶפְסֵדוֹ בִּשְׂכָרוֹ; מָהִיר לִשְׁמֽוֹעַ וְקָשֶׁה לְאַבֵּד, זֶה חֵֽלֶק טוֹב; קָשֶׁה לִשְׁמֽוֹעַ וּמָהִיר לְאַבֵּד, זֶה חֵֽלֶק רָע.

[טז] אַרְבַּע מִדּוֹת בְּנוֹתְנֵי צְדָקָה: הָרוֹצֶה שֶׁיִּתֵּן וְלֹא יִתְּנוּ אֲחֵרִים, עֵינוֹ רָעָה בְּשֶׁל אֲחֵרִים; יִתְּנוּ אֲחֵרִים וְהוּא לֹא יִתֵּן, עֵינוֹ רָעָה בְּשֶׁלּוֹ; יִתֵּן וְיִתְּנוּ אֲחֵרִים, חָסִיד; לֹא יִתֵּן וְלֹא יִתְּנוּ אֲחֵרִים, רָשָׁע.

---

14. יָצָא שְׂכָרוֹ בְּהֶפְסֵדוֹ — **He loses more . . . than he gains.**
Even though he tries to make up for his anger, he can never erase the things he said and did while he was angry. For example: An angry person told his friend, "I hate you!" Later he apologized and asked forgiveness. Even when his friend forgives him, it will be very difficult for the friend to forget the angry remark.

15. זֶה חֵֽלֶק טוֹב — **He has a good portion.**
In *mishnayos* 13,14,16 and 17 we find the words חָסִיד, *chassid*, and רָשָׁע, *wicked*. But here we have "a good portion" and "a bad portion." The difference is simple. A person can train himself to practice good *middos*. If he does, he is a good person. If his *middos* are extra special, he is a *chassid*. Similarly, a person with very bad *middos* is wicked.

But intelligence is not the same as other *middos*. Before a person is born, *Hashem* determines whether that person will be wise or not, whether he will have deep understanding or will find learning new things difficult. Therefore, when the *mishnah* speaks about a good memory and a poor memory, it uses the word "portion." A good mind is a good portion and should be used to make its owner a great person. And a poor mind is a bad portion, but its owner still should never give up trying to learn. Even if he is not successful, it is not his fault, and *Hashem* rewards him for trying.

16. עֵינוֹ רָעָה בְּשֶׁל אֲחֵרִים — **He sees others in a bad way.**
This means that he does not want them to do the right thing.

17. There are four ways people act about going to the *beis midrash* to study Torah: (a) If a person goes to the *beis midrash*, but does not study there — that person gets a reward for going. (b) If a person does not go to the *beis midrash*, but studies at home — that person gets a reward for studying. (c) If a person goes to the *beis midrash*, and studies there — that person is a *chassid*. (d) If a person does not go to the *beis midrash*, and does not study at home — that person is wicked.

18. There are four types of students who sit before the Sages: (a) a sponge; (b) a funnel; (c) a strainer; (d) a sieve.

(a) A sponge absorbs everything. (b) A funnel takes in from one end and lets out from the other end. (c) A strainer lets the wine flow through and holds back the waste. (d) A sieve takes out the coarse meal and collects the fine flour.

[יז] אַרְבַּע מִדּוֹת בְּהוֹלְכֵי בֵית הַמִּדְרָשׁ: הוֹלֵךְ וְאֵינוֹ עוֹשֶׂה, שְׂכַר הֲלִיכָה בְּיָדוֹ; עוֹשֶׂה וְאֵינוֹ הוֹלֵךְ, שְׂכַר מַעֲשֶׂה בְּיָדוֹ; הוֹלֵךְ וְעוֹשֶׂה, חָסִיד; לֹא הוֹלֵךְ וְלֹא עוֹשֶׂה, רָשָׁע.

[יח] אַרְבַּע מִדּוֹת בְּיוֹשְׁבִים לִפְנֵי חֲכָמִים: סְפוֹג, וּמַשְׁפֵּךְ, מְשַׁמֶּרֶת, וְנָפָה. סְפוֹג, שֶׁהוּא סוֹפֵג אֶת הַכֹּל; וּמַשְׁפֵּךְ, שֶׁמַּכְנִיס בְּזוֹ וּמוֹצִיא בְזוֹ; מְשַׁמֶּרֶת, שֶׁמּוֹצִיאָה אֶת הַיַּיִן וְקוֹלֶטֶת אֶת הַשְּׁמָרִים; וְנָפָה, שֶׁמּוֹצִיאָה אֶת הַקֶּמַח וְקוֹלֶטֶת אֶת הַסֹּלֶת.

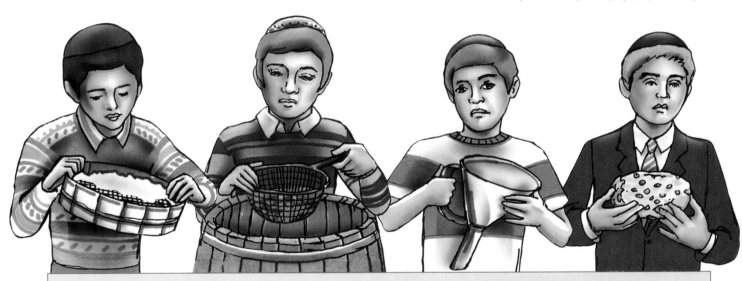

18. בְּיוֹשְׁבִים לִפְנֵי חֲכָמִים — **Of students who sit before the Sages.**

Mishnah 15 also describes four types of students. But that *mishnah* speaks about memory, while our *mishnah* speaks about understanding what is taught.

Not everything that is taught is important. Some facts may not be very important by themselves, but the teacher uses them to make the students think.

Some students are like sponges. A sponge soaks up all kinds of liquid — fresh or stale. In the sponge, the fresh and stale join together and all the liquid becomes spoiled. Such students remember everything they hear, but they do not know what is important and what is not. They remember all the facts, but they jumble them all together, so they cannot use their knowledge well. They will be able to repeat all the information they have learned. But it will make no sense.

Other students are like funnels. What goes into one end of the funnel comes out of the other. These students memorize everything exactly as they heard it, and they repeat it in the exact same way. Nothing gets changed or improved by passing through their minds.

Some students are like wine strainers that let the good wine flow through into its container, and hold back the waste, such as the grapeskins and pits. These students think that the unimportant facts are important, and the important facts are unimportant. So they keep stressing the unimportant things.

Finally, there are the best students who are like sieves that collect the finest flour and keep all the less valuable meal out. These are the wise students who use the facts they are taught in a proper way. They build ideas and develop their minds. Whatever is necessary for them to know, they remember. But what is not important, they allow to slip out of their heads.

19. If a person loves another person for only one special reason, then if that reason disappears, the love will also disappear. But if a person loves another person not just for one special reason, then that love will never disappear.

What is an example of love for only one special reason? The love that Amnon had for Tamar (*Shmuel II* 13:1). And what is an example of love not for just one special reason? The brotherly love of David and Yehonasan.

20. If an argument is for the sake of Heaven, and both sides try to discover the truth, then the truth learned through that argument will last forever. But if an argument is not for the sake of Heaven, and one side just tries to win even if it is wrong, then nothing of that argument will last.

What is an example of arguments that are for the sake of Heaven? The arguments between Hillel and Shammai. And what is an example of arguments that are not for the sake of Heaven? The arguments of Korach and his followers against Moshe *Rabbeinu*.

21. If any person causes many people to do *mitzvos*, no sin will be caused by that person. And if any person causes other people to sin, that person will never be given the chance to do *teshuvah*.

Moshe *Rabbeinu* did *mitzvos* and caused many people to do *mitzvos*, so their *mitzvos* are counted as if they were his — as it is written in the Torah (*Deuteronomy* 33:21), "He did *Hashem's* good deeds, and His laws together with Israel."

Yeravam ben Nevat sinned and caused many people to sin, so their sins are counted as if they were his — as it is written (*Melachim I* 15:30), "For the sins of Yeravam, for he sinned and he caused Israel to sin."

[יט] כָּל אַהֲבָה שֶׁהִיא תְלוּיָה בְדָבָר, בָּטֵל דָּבָר, בְּטֵלָה אַהֲבָה; וְשֶׁאֵינָה תְלוּיָה בְדָבָר, אֵינָה בְּטֵלָה לְעוֹלָם. אֵיזוֹ הִיא אַהֲבָה שֶׁהִיא תְלוּיָה בְדָבָר? זוֹ אַהֲבַת אַמְנוֹן וְתָמָר. וְשֶׁאֵינָה תְלוּיָה בְדָבָר? זוֹ אַהֲבַת דָּוִד וִיהוֹנָתָן.

[כ] כָּל מַחֲלֹקֶת שֶׁהִיא לְשֵׁם שָׁמַיִם, סוֹפָה לְהִתְקַיֵּם; וְשֶׁאֵינָה לְשֵׁם שָׁמַיִם, אֵין סוֹפָה לְהִתְקַיֵּם. אֵיזוֹ הִיא מַחֲלֹקֶת שֶׁהִיא לְשֵׁם שָׁמַיִם? זוֹ מַחֲלֹקֶת הִלֵּל וְשַׁמַּאי. וְשֶׁאֵינָה לְשֵׁם שָׁמַיִם? זוֹ מַחֲלֹקֶת קֹרַח וְכָל עֲדָתוֹ.

[כא] כָּל הַמְזַכֶּה אֶת הָרַבִּים, אֵין חֵטְא בָּא עַל יָדוֹ; וְכָל הַמַּחֲטִיא אֶת הָרַבִּים, אֵין מַסְפִּיקִין בְּיָדוֹ לַעֲשׂוֹת תְּשׁוּבָה. מֹשֶׁה זָכָה וְזִכָּה אֶת הָרַבִּים, זְכוּת הָרַבִּים תָּלוּי בּוֹ, שֶׁנֶּאֱמַר: "צִדְקַת יהוה עָשָׂה, וּמִשְׁפָּטָיו עִם יִשְׂרָאֵל." יָרָבְעָם בֶּן נְבָט חָטָא וְהֶחֱטִיא אֶת הָרַבִּים, חֵטְא הָרַבִּים תָּלוּי בּוֹ, שֶׁנֶּאֱמַר: "עַל חַטֹּאות יָרָבְעָם אֲשֶׁר חָטָא, וַאֲשֶׁר הֶחֱטִיא אֶת יִשְׂרָאֵל."

---

19. אַהֲבַת דָּוִד וִיהוֹנָתָן — **The brotherly love of David and Yehonasan.**

Shaul *Hamelech* was the first king appointed over israel. When Shaul was anointed, Shmuel *Hanavi* gave him special instructions (*Shmuel I* 10:8). Unfortunately, Shaul was unable to carry out these instructions the right way. Shmuel told Shaul that because of this, his son will not become king after him. The ruler after Shaul would be from a different family (13:8-14). Later, Shmuel *Hanavi* revealed that David the son of Yishai would become king after Shaul.

Yehonasan was the son of Shaul. If his father had followed the prophet's instructions properly, Yehonasan would have been the next king. He had every reason to be jealous of David and to hate him. But he didn't. Yehonasan realized what a great person David was. He understood why David was chosen to become the king. And he loved David like a brother. As the *Navi* states (18:1), "Yehonasan's soul was bound to David's soul, and Yehonasan loved him as himself."

20. מַחֲלֹקֶת הִלֵּל וְשַׁמַּאי — **The arguments between Hillel and Shammai.**

Hillel and Shammai, as well as their *yeshivos* (Beis Hillel and Beis Shammai), often argued over questions of *halachah* — one said, "Kosher," the other said, "Treif"; one said, "This act is permitted," the other said, "It is forbidden." Each side brought verses and arguments to prove its point. Although each side tried to prove that it was right, the important thing about these arguments is that neither side wanted to win just for the sake of winning. They only wanted to discover the true *halachah*. That is why the discussions of Hillel and Shammai are studied to this very day by students in *yeshivos* all over the world. They are not studied as arguments that have losers and winners. Both are winners. The words of Hillel, Shammai and their students are a part of the Oral Torah (see chapter 3, *mishnah* 17). And even though the *halachah* almost always follows Beis Hillel, we study Beis Shammai's reasons and proofs, just as we study Beis Hillel's.

But Korach and his followers argued with Moshe *Rabbeinu* for a different reason. They were jealous of Moshe *Rabbeinu* and his brother Aharon *Hakohein*. They wanted to become the leaders. They did not care for the truth; they only cared for themselves. So when we study about them in the Torah, we do not try to learn from their ways. Instead we use them as examples of people with bad *middos*.

Avraham Avinu

The wicked Bilam

22. Anyone who acts in three certain ways is among the students of Avraham *Avinu.* And anyone who acts in three opposite ways is among the students of the wicked Bilam.

A good eye, a humble spirit, and a modest soul are the ways of Avraham *Avinu's* students. A bad eye, an arrogant spirit, and a greedy soul are the ways of the wicked Bilam's students.

What is the difference between what will happen to Avraham *Avinu's* students and what will happen to the wicked Bilam's students? Avraham *Avinu's* students will have their reward in this world and will inherit the World to Come — as Shlomo *Hamelech* wrote (*Mishlei* 8:21), "God says: 'I will give those who love Me an inheritance in the World to Come, and I will fill their storehouses in this world.'" But the students of the wicked Bilam will inherit *Gehinnom* and will go down into the Well of Destruction — as David *Hamelech* wrote (*Tehillim* 55:24), "You, O God, will lower them into the Well of Destruction; these murderers and liars will not live for even half of the years they were supposed to live; but I will trust in You."

[כב] כָּל מִי שֶׁיֵּשׁ בְּיָדוֹ שְׁלֹשָׁה דְבָרִים הַלָּלוּ, הוּא מִתַּלְמִידָיו שֶׁל אַבְרָהָם אָבִינוּ; וּשְׁלֹשָׁה דְבָרִים אֲחֵרִים, הוּא מִתַּלְמִידָיו שֶׁל בִּלְעָם הָרָשָׁע. עַיִן טוֹבָה, וְרוּחַ נְמוּכָה, וְנֶפֶשׁ שְׁפָלָה, תַּלְמִידָיו שֶׁל אַבְרָהָם אָבִינוּ. עַיִן רָעָה, וְרוּחַ גְּבוֹהָה, וְנֶפֶשׁ רְחָבָה, תַּלְמִידָיו שֶׁל בִּלְעָם הָרָשָׁע. מַה בֵּין תַּלְמִידָיו שֶׁל אַבְרָהָם אָבִינוּ לְתַלְמִידָיו שֶׁל בִּלְעָם הָרָשָׁע? תַּלְמִידָיו שֶׁל אַבְרָהָם אָבִינוּ אוֹכְלִין בָּעוֹלָם הַזֶּה, וְנוֹחֲלִין הָעוֹלָם הַבָּא, שֶׁנֶּאֱמַר: "לְהַנְחִיל אֹהֲבַי יֵשׁ, וְאֹצְרֹתֵיהֶם אֲמַלֵּא." אֲבָל תַּלְמִידָיו שֶׁל בִּלְעָם הָרָשָׁע יוֹרְשִׁין גֵּיהִנֹּם, וְיוֹרְדִין לִבְאֵר שָׁחַת, שֶׁנֶּאֱמַר: "וְאַתָּה אֱלֹהִים תּוֹרִדֵם לִבְאֵר שַׁחַת, אַנְשֵׁי דָמִים וּמִרְמָה לֹא יֶחֱצוּ יְמֵיהֶם, וַאֲנִי אֶבְטַח בָּךְ."

23. Yehudah ben Teima taught:

Be bold as a leopard, light as an eagle, fast as a deer, and strong as a lion, to do the *mitzvos* of your Father in Heaven.

[כג] יְהוּדָה בֶּן תֵּימָא אוֹמֵר: הֱוֵי עַז כַּנָּמֵר, וְקַל כַּנֶּשֶׁר, רָץ כַּצְּבִי, וְגִבּוֹר כָּאֲרִי לַעֲשׂוֹת רְצוֹן אָבִיךָ שֶׁבַּשָּׁמָיִם.

23-24. הֱוֵי עַז כַּנָּמֵר . . . עַז פָּנִים לְגֵיהִנֹּם — **Be bold as a leopard. . . A bold-faced person will go to Gehinnom.**

Yehudah ben Teima seems to contradict himself. First he tells us to be bold as a leopard. That means boldness is a good *middah*. Then he says that bold-faced people end up in *Gehinnom*. That means boldness is a bad *middah*! How can we understand these two lessons?

Middos can sometimes be "good" and sometimes be "bad." Love, joy and kindness are usually called "good" *middos*. Anger, hate and laziness are usually called "bad" *middos*. But are these *middos* really either completely good or completely bad? For example, is joy in doing a sin good or bad? Is a mother's anger bad when her child misbehaves?

Let us study the word מִדָּה, *middah*, for a moment. The original meaning of this word is "measure." Inches and miles, pounds and ounces, minutes and hours, all these are *middos* or measures. Can an ounce of salt be good or bad? That depends on what you use it for. If you try eating an egg with an ounce of salt, you will say that an ounce of salt is terrible. But when your mother cooks a very large pot of chicken soup for the family and *Shabbos* guests, an ounce of salt may be just perfect. So *middos* (measures) are not really good or bad. It depends on the size of the "measure" and how it is used.

The same is true about the feelings and actions which are also called *middos*. Each *middah* must be used in the proper amount, at the proper time, and for the proper reason. We should not use the "good" *middah* of joy when we see a sin

being done. And we should use the "bad" *middah* of stinginess when someone tries to sell us useless, foolish things.

These are the lessons of Yehudah ben Teima. עַזּוּת, *boldness*, is necessary when performing *mitzvos*. When we follow the ways of the Torah, we should be bold — even if other people laugh at us. Such boldness is a good *middah*. But we also must be careful not to let *boldness* become a part of everything we do. If a person acts boldly in everything he does, he will soon become arrogant and boastful. Such boldness is a bad *middah*.

יְהִי רָצוֹן . . . — **May it be Your will . . .**

This passage seems strangely out of place. It is not a lesson in *middos*. It is a prayer for the rebuilding of the *Beis Hamikdash* and for us to have a share in the Torah. In fact, this is the only prayer that we find in all of the sixty-three *masechtos*, or volumes, of the *Mishnah*. This is the kind of prayer we find at the end of a *masechta*. In fact, this prayer does appear at the end of the section of *Shacharis* that describes the *korbanos*, and again at the end of *Shemoneh Esrei*.

Actually, this *mishnah* was once the end of *Pirkei Avos*. The last two *mishnayos* of this chapter and the whole sixth chapter were part of the *Maseches Kallah*, which was written during the same time period as the *Mishnah*. That is why this prayer appears here. (At the beginning of chapter six we will explain why that chapter was added.)

24. He used to teach:

A bold-faced person will go to *Gehinnom*, and a shame-faced person will go to *Gan Eden*.

May it be Your will — Hashem, our God and the God of our fathers — to allow the *Beis Hamikdash* to be built again, soon, in our lifetime, and to give us a share in Your Torah.

25. (He used to teach:)

A five-year-old should already have started to study *Tanach*. A ten-year-old should already have started to study *Mishnah*. A thirteen-year-old is an adult and is required to keep all the *mitzvos*. A fifteen-year-old should already have started to study *Gemara*. An eighteen-year-old has reached the age to marry. A twenty-year-old begins to earn a livelihood. A thirty-year-old has reached his full strength. A forty-year-old has reached the age of understanding. A fifty-year-old has reached the age of giving advice. A sixty-year-old has reached the age of wisdom. A seventy-year-old has reached a ripe old age. An eighty-year-old has reached the age of spiritual strength. A ninety-year-old has reached the age when his body is bent over. A hundred-year-old has reached the age when most people have died and left this world.

26. Ben Bag Bag taught:

You should study the Torah from all sides and you will always turn up new knowledge, because all the wisdom of this world is in the Torah. You should look into it all of your lifetime and grow old and gray with it. You should never move away from it, for there is nothing in the world that is better than the Torah.

Ben Hei Hei taught:

Your reward for doing *mitzvos* will be according to your pain and your effort.

[כד] הוּא הָיָה אוֹמֵר:

עַז פָּנִים לְגֵיהִנֹּם, וּבֹשֶׁת פָּנִים לְגַן עֵדֶן. יְהִי רָצוֹן מִלְּפָנֶיךָ יהוה אֱלֹהֵינוּ וֵאלֹהֵי אֲבוֹתֵינוּ שֶׁיִּבָּנֶה בֵּית הַמִּקְדָּשׁ בִּמְהֵרָה בְיָמֵינוּ וְתֵן חֶלְקֵנוּ בְּתוֹרָתֶךָ.

[כה] הוּא הָיָה אוֹמֵר:

בֶּן חָמֵשׁ שָׁנִים לַמִּקְרָא, בֶּן עֶשֶׂר שָׁנִים לַמִּשְׁנָה, בֶּן שְׁלֹשׁ עֶשְׂרֵה לַמִּצְוֹת, בֶּן חֲמֵשׁ עֶשְׂרֵה לַגְּמָרָא, בֶּן שְׁמוֹנֶה עֶשְׂרֵה לַחֻפָּה, בֶּן עֶשְׂרִים לִרְדּוֹף, בֶּן שְׁלֹשִׁים לַכֹּחַ, בֶּן אַרְבָּעִים לַבִּינָה, בֶּן חֲמִשִּׁים לְעֵצָה, בֶּן שִׁשִּׁים לְזִקְנָה, בֶּן שִׁבְעִים לְשֵׂיבָה, בֶּן שְׁמוֹנִים לִגְבוּרָה, בֶּן תִּשְׁעִים לָשׁוּחַ, בֶּן מֵאָה כְּאִלּוּ מֵת וְעָבַר וּבָטֵל מִן הָעוֹלָם.

[כו] בֶּן בַּג בַּג אוֹמֵר:

הֲפָךְ בָּהּ וַהֲפָךְ בָּהּ, דְּכֹלָּא בָהּ; וּבָהּ תֶּחֱזֵי, וְסִיב וּבְלֵה בָהּ, וּמִנַּהּ לָא תָזוּעַ, שֶׁאֵין לְךָ מִדָּה טוֹבָה הֵימֶנָּה. בֶּן הֵא הֵא אוֹמֵר: לְפוּם צַעֲרָא אַגְרָא.

---

25. בֶּן שְׁלֹשׁ עֶשְׂרֵה לַמִּצְוֹת — **A thirteen-year-old is an adult and is required to keep all the mitzvos.**

This does not mean that a child does not have to keep the *mitzvos*. A child must be taught Torah, *mitzvos*, charity, kindness and all other good *middos* at a very young age. Of course, each thing must be taught at the proper time. That's why the Torah assigns different ages for studying *Tanach*, *Mishnah* and *Gemara*.

When you are a child, you often must be reminded about *mitzvos* — "It's still *Shabbos*, so we may not turn on the light yet!" — "I think you forgot to say a *berachah* on that apple." — "We had meat for lunch, so the ice cream will have to wait until later." — "Would you like to show

Mommy how you put money in the *tzedakah pushka?*" But when we reach the age of thirteen, we become mature enough so that we shouldn't need reminders any more. That is why, as young adults, we are responsible for doing the *mitzvos* on our own.

The age of thirteen in this *mishnah* has two meanings. A girl becomes mature earlier than a boy does, a whole year earlier. And on her twelfth birthday, which is really the first day of her thirteenth year, she becomes an adult. From that day on she is responsible for her own *mitzvos*. A boy, however, becomes mature later. So a boy becomes an adult, responsible for his own *mitzvos*, on his thirteenth birthday.

he Sages taught this chapter as if it were a part of the *Mishnah*. Blessed is *Hashem* Who chose them and their teaching.

1. R' Meir taught:

When you study Torah because that is what *Hashem* wants you to do, then you earn many things. Not only do you earn a great reward, but the creation of the whole world was worthwhile just so that you should study Torah. You will be called "Friend" and "Beloved." You will learn to love God and to love His creatures. You will make God happy and His creatures happy. The Torah will dress you in the robes of humbleness and fear of God. It will prepare you to become a *tzaddik*, a *chassid*, a fair and reliable person. It will keep you far away from sin, and bring you close to merit. People will enjoy your advice, wisdom, understanding and spiritual strength — as Shlomo *Hamelech* said of the Torah (*Mishlei* 8:14), "Advice and wisdom are mine; I am understanding; strength is mine." The Torah will give you royalty, rulership, and understanding of the law. The secrets of the Torah will be opened for you. You will keep becoming wiser and wiser, like a fountain that flows more and more, and like an endless river. The Torah will teach you to be modest, patient, and to forgive people who insult you. And it will make you greater and raise you higher than everything else in the world.

שָׁנוּ חֲכָמִים בִּלְשׁוֹן הַמִּשְׁנָה. בָּרוּךְ שֶׁבָּחַר בָּהֶם וּבְמִשְׁנָתָם.

[א] רַבִּי מֵאִיר אוֹמֵר:

כָּל הָעוֹסֵק בַּתּוֹרָה לִשְׁמָהּ זוֹכֶה לִדְבָרִים הַרְבֵּה; וְלֹא עוֹד, אֶלָּא שֶׁכָּל הָעוֹלָם כֻּלּוֹ כְּדַאי הוּא לוֹ. נִקְרָא רֵעַ, אָהוּב. אוֹהֵב אֶת הַמָּקוֹם, אוֹהֵב אֶת הַבְּרִיּוֹת, מְשַׂמֵּחַ אֶת הַמָּקוֹם, מְשַׂמֵּחַ אֶת הַבְּרִיּוֹת. וּמַלְבַּשְׁתּוֹ עֲנָוָה וְיִרְאָה; וּמַכְשַׁרְתּוֹ לִהְיוֹת צַדִּיק, חָסִיד, יָשָׁר, וְנֶאֱמָן; וּמְרַחַקְתּוֹ מִן הַחֵטְא, וּמְקָרַבְתּוֹ לִידֵי זְכוּת. וְנֶהֱנִין מִמֶּנּוּ עֵצָה וְתוּשִׁיָּה, בִּינָה וּגְבוּרָה, שֶׁנֶּאֱמַר: "לִי עֵצָה וְתוּשִׁיָּה, אֲנִי בִינָה, לִי גְבוּרָה." וְנוֹתֶנֶת לוֹ מַלְכוּת, וּמֶמְשָׁלָה, וְחִקּוּר דִּין; וּמְגַלִּין לוֹ רָזֵי תוֹרָה; וְנַעֲשֶׂה כְּמַעְיָן הַמִּתְגַּבֵּר, וּכְנָהָר שֶׁאֵינוֹ פוֹסֵק; וְהֹוֶה צָנוּעַ, וְאֶרֶךְ רוּחַ, וּמוֹחֵל עַל עֶלְבּוֹנוֹ. וּמְגַדַּלְתּוֹ וּמְרוֹמַמְתּוֹ עַל כָּל הַמַּעֲשִׂים.

בִּלְשׁוֹן הַמִּשְׁנָה — **As if it were a part of the Mishnah.**
The Rabbis who taught the *Mishnah* were called *Tannaim*. Many of their teachings were gathered by R' Yehudah *Hanassi* into the *Mishnah*. But R' Yehudah did not include all of their teachings. Many of them were gathered later into other collections called *baraisos*. One of those collections is called *Kallah Rabbasi*. And the sixth chapter of *Avos* is really the eighth chapter of *Kallah Rabbasi*. So even though this chapter was not included in the *Mishnah* by R' Yehudah, it contains lessons from the *Tannaim*, and we may consider it "as if it were a part of the *Mishnah*."
At first, *Avos* had only five chapters. Many centuries after the *Mishnah* was written, people began to study and recite the chapters of *Avos* in the weeks between *Pesach* and *Shavuos*, one chapter for each of the first five *Shabbosos*. On the sixth *Shabbos* they would study the eighth chapter of *Kallah Rabbasi*, because it discusses the importance of learning Torah. For this reason it is the fitting chapter to study on the *Shabbos* before *Shavuos*, the *Yom Tov* when

Hashem gave the Torah on Mount Sinai. After a while, the printers began printing this chapter at the end of *Avos*, and it did not take long before it became known as the sixth chapter of *Avos*.

1. זוֹכֶה לִדְבָרִים הַרְבֵּה — **Then you earn many things.**
A person who studies Torah on a regular schedule gets so many blessings that it would be impossible to list them. So the *Tanna* lists only some of them in this *mishnah*, but he wants us to know that there are many other blessings. Therefore the *Tanna* says that there are דְבָרִים הַרְבֵּה, *many things*.

צַדִּיק חָסִיד — **A tzaddik, a chassid.**
This is the difference between a *tzaddik* and a *chassid*: A *tzaddik* follows the *halachah* exactly. He is careful never to do anything wrong and he is careful to do all the *mitzvos*. But a *chassid* goes further. He does more than the *halachah* says that he must do. We can understand this better with an example.

The creation of the whole world was worthwhile just so that you should study Torah.

Reuvain and Shimon are classmates. They are both good students. At the beginning of the school year their *rebbi* said that every night each student should spend at least twenty minutes reviewing *Mishnayos* after completing all his written homework. Reuvain follows this rule carefully. Every night as soon as he puts away his notebooks, Reuvain takes out his *Mishnayos* and studies for exactly twenty minutes. No more, no less.

Shimon also studies *Mishnayos* after completing his written assignment each night. He studies for twenty minutes, or thirty, sometimes even for an hour. And his friends know that they can call him to ask questions when they need help. Both Reuvain and Shimon are good students. Both will know their *mishnayos*. Both will be praised by their *rebbi*. But one does more than the other.

Like Reuvain following his *rebbi's* instructions, the *tzaddik* does exactly what the *halachah* says he must do. But the *chassid*, like Shimon, does much more than the *halachah* requires. Both are good people. Both will receive their rewards in *Olam Haba*. But one will receive a greater reward than the other.

2. R' Yehoshua ben Levi taught:

Every single day, a heavenly voice calls out from Mount Sinai and proclaims, "Woe to the people, because they insult the Torah!" Whoever does not study Torah is considered banned — and is the type of person described by Shlomo *Hamelech* (*Mishlei* 11:22), "Like a golden ring in a pig's nose, a beautiful woman who acts foolishly."

Even more, the Torah describes the *Luchos* on which the Ten Commandments were written (*Shemos* 32:16), "The *Luchos* are God's work, and the writing is God's writing engraved (חָרוּת) upon the *Luchos*." Do not read only חָרוּת, *engraved*, but also חֵרוּת, *freedom*. This teaches that the only truly free person is one who studies the Torah. And anyone who studies the Torah is raised to a higher level — as the Torah says, (*Bamidbar* 21:19), "From Mattanah to Nachaliel, and from Nachaliel to Bamos."

3. If you learn Torah from your friend — even one chapter, one *halachah*, one Torah verse, one Torah word, or even just one letter — you must treat him with honor. For we find that David, the King of the Jewish People, only learned two things from Achisofel, yet David considered him as his teacher, his guide and his close advisor — as he wrote about Achisofel in *Tehillim* (55:14), "You are a man who is equal to me, my guide and my close advisor."

Now we may certainly learn a lesson from this. If David, King of Israel, learned only two things from Achisofel, and yet considered him as his teacher, his guide and his close advisor, then certainly an ordinary person who learns anything from his friend — one chapter, one *halachah*, one Torah verse, one Torah word, or even just one letter — must treat his friend with honor.

True honor is gained only by studying Torah — as it says in *Mishlei* (3:35), "Wise people shall inherit honor," and (28:10), "Perfect people shall inherit good." And only the Torah is truly good — as it says (4:2), "I have given you a good portion, My Torah, do not forsake it."

[ב] אָמַר רַבִּי יְהוֹשֻׁעַ בֶּן לֵוִי:

בְּכָל יוֹם וָיוֹם בַּת קוֹל יוֹצֵאת מֵהַר חוֹרֵב, וּמַכְרֶזֶת וְאוֹמֶרֶת: "אוֹי לָהֶם לַבְּרִיּוֹת, מֵעֶלְבּוֹנָהּ שֶׁל תּוֹרָה!" שֶׁכָּל מִי שֶׁאֵינוֹ עוֹסֵק בַּתּוֹרָה נִקְרָא נָזוּף, שֶׁנֶּאֱמַר: "נֶזֶם זָהָב בְּאַף חֲזִיר, אִשָּׁה יָפָה וְסָרַת טָעַם."

וְאוֹמֵר: "וְהַלֻּחֹת מַעֲשֵׂה אֱלֹהִים הֵמָּה וְהַמִּכְתָּב מִכְתַּב אֱלֹהִים הוּא חָרוּת עַל הַלֻּחֹת." אַל תִּקְרָא "חָרוּת" אֶלָּא "חֵרוּת," שֶׁאֵין לְךָ בֶּן חֹרִין אֶלָּא מִי שֶׁעוֹסֵק בְּתַלְמוּד תּוֹרָה. וְכָל מִי שֶׁעוֹסֵק בְּתַלְמוּד תּוֹרָה הֲרֵי זֶה מִתְעַלֶּה, שֶׁנֶּאֱמַר: "וּמִמַּתָּנָה נַחֲלִיאֵל, וּמִנַּחֲלִיאֵל בָּמוֹת."

[ג] הַלּוֹמֵד מֵחֲבֵרוֹ פֶּרֶק אֶחָד, אוֹ הֲלָכָה אַחַת, אוֹ פָּסוּק אֶחָד, אוֹ דִבּוּר אֶחָד, אוֹ אֲפִילוּ אוֹת אַחַת — צָרִיךְ לִנְהֹג בּוֹ כָּבוֹד. שֶׁכֵּן מָצִינוּ בְּדָוִד מֶלֶךְ יִשְׂרָאֵל, שֶׁלֹּא לָמַד מֵאֲחִיתֹפֶל אֶלָּא שְׁנֵי דְבָרִים בִּלְבַד, וּקְרָאוֹ רַבּוֹ, אַלּוּפוֹ, וּמְיֻדָּעוֹ, שֶׁנֶּאֱמַר: "וְאַתָּה אֱנוֹשׁ כְּעֶרְכִּי, אַלּוּפִי וּמְיֻדָּעִי."

וַהֲלֹא דְבָרִים קַל וָחֹמֶר: וּמַה דָּוִד מֶלֶךְ יִשְׂרָאֵל, שֶׁלֹּא לָמַד מֵאֲחִיתֹפֶל אֶלָּא שְׁנֵי דְבָרִים בִּלְבַד, קְרָאוֹ רַבּוֹ אַלּוּפוֹ וּמְיֻדָּעוֹ — הַלּוֹמֵד מֵחֲבֵרוֹ פֶּרֶק אֶחָד, אוֹ הֲלָכָה אַחַת, אוֹ פָּסוּק אֶחָד, אוֹ דִבּוּר אֶחָד, אוֹ אֲפִילוּ אוֹת אַחַת, עַל אַחַת כַּמָּה וְכַמָּה שֶׁצָּרִיךְ לִנְהֹג בּוֹ כָּבוֹד!

וְאֵין כָּבוֹד אֶלָּא תּוֹרָה, שֶׁנֶּאֱמַר: "כָּבוֹד חֲכָמִים יִנְחָלוּ"; "וּתְמִימִים יִנְחֲלוּ טוֹב." וְאֵין טוֹב אֶלָּא תּוֹרָה, שֶׁנֶּאֱמַר: "כִּי לֶקַח טוֹב נָתַתִּי לָכֶם, תּוֹרָתִי אַל תַּעֲזֹבוּ."

---

2. נָזוּף — **Banned.**

"Banned" means "locked out." A person banned by a school may not enter that school. A person banned by a king will not be allowed to enter the royal palace. Someone who does not study Torah is considered נָזוּף, *banned*, by God.

We learn this from the sentence in *Mishlei*. The Torah is a נֶזֶם זָהָב, *golden ring*, that was given to every Jew. It will decorate and beautify anyone who studies it and keeps its *mitzvos*. But if a person ignores the Torah he disgraces it, like a golden ring בְּאַף חֲזִיר, *in a pig's nose*. The ring is

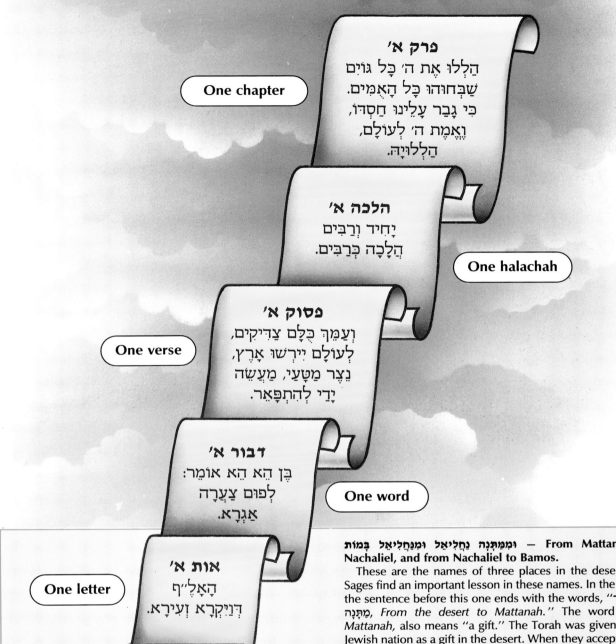

One chapter

פרק א׳
הַלְלוּ אֶת ה׳ כָּל גּוֹיִם
שַׁבְּחוּהוּ כָּל הָאֻמִּים.
כִּי גָבַר עָלֵינוּ חַסְדּוֹ,
וֶאֱמֶת ה׳ לְעוֹלָם,
הַלְלוּיָהּ.

One halachah

הלכה א׳
יָחִיד וְרַבִּים
הֲלָכָה כְּרַבִּים.

One verse

פסוק א׳
וְעַמֵּךְ כֻּלָּם צַדִּיקִים,
לְעוֹלָם יִירְשׁוּ אָרֶץ,
נֵצֶר מַטָּעַי, מַעֲשֵׂה
יָדַי לְהִתְפָּאֵר.

One word

דבור א׳
בֶּן הֵא הֵא אוֹמֵר:
לְפוּם צַעֲרָא
אַגְרָא.

One letter

אות א׳
הָאָלֶ״ף
דְּנַיְקְרָא זְעֵירָא.

beautiful and valuable, but the pig will poke it in the garbage and make it filthy. The word נָזוּף, *banned,* is an abbreviation for נֶזֶם זָהָב בְּאַף חֲזִיר, *a golden ring in a pig's nose.* This teaches us that a person who doesn't study Torah is not making proper use of *Hashem's* special gift.

אַל תִּקְרָא ״חָרוּת״ אֶלָּא ״חֵרוּת״ — **Do not read only** חָרוּת, **engraved, but also** חֵרוּת**, freedom.**

This does not mean that we wish to change the word חָרוּת in the Torah. Nobody can ever change a single word in the Torah. It means that since the Torah is written without vowels, we can interpret words in more than one way. In this case we take the words חָרוּת עַל הַלֻּחֹת, *engraved upon the Luchos,* and also read them חֵרוּת עַל הַלֻּחֹת, *freedom is on the Luchos.* In other words, if a person wishes to be truly free from his *yetzer hara,* he must study the Torah that was given on the *Luchos* at Mount Sinai.

וּמִמַּתָּנָה נַחֲלִיאֵל וּמִנַּחֲלִיאֵל בָּמוֹת — **From Mattanah to Nachaliel, and from Nachaliel to Bamos.**

These are the names of three places in the desert. The Sages find an important lesson in these names. In the Torah, the sentence before this one ends with the words, ״וּמִמִּדְבָּר מַתָּנָה, *From the desert to Mattanah.''* The word מַתָּנָה, *Mattanah,* also means ''a gift.'' The Torah was given to the Jewish nation as a gift in the desert. When they accepted the Torah, they became נַחֲלִיאֵל, which is made up of the two words נַחֲלִי אֵל, *the heritage (or possession) of God.* And when they study Torah they are placed on בָּמוֹת, *high places.* That means that *Hashem* gives them great honor.

3. שְׁנֵי דְבָרִים בִּלְבָד — **Only two things.**

After the sentence, "You are a man who is equal to me, my guide and my close advisor," David *Hamelech* said, ״אֲשֶׁר יַחְדָּו נַמְתִּיק סוֹד, *Together we would learn sweet secrets;* בְּבֵית אֱלֹקִים נְהַלֵּךְ בְּרָגֶשׁ, *in God's House we would walk briskly.''* This sentence contains the two lessons that Achisofel taught David *Hamelech.* One time Achisofel saw the king studying Torah by himself. He told David *Hamelech* that it is better to study Torah with a partner — as it says, "**Together** we would learn sweet secrets." Another time Achisofel saw David *Hamelech* entering the *beis midrash* slowly. He told the king that a person should walk briskly when he was going to the *beis midrash* — as it says, "In God's House we would walk **briskly.**"

4. This is the way of Torah study: Even if you have nothing to eat except bread with salt, even if you have nothing to drink except a small amount of water, even if you have no place to sleep except on the ground, even if your whole life is full of hardship, you should still work hard at learning Torah. If you do this, then you will earn the description given in *Tehillim* (128:2), ''You deserve praise and all is well with you.'' This means ''you deserve praise'' in this world, and ''all is well with you'' in the World to Come.

5. You should not seek a high position for yourself, and you should not desire honor, but you should try to do more *mitzvos* than you are used to doing. Do not yearn to sit at the kings' table, because your table is greater than theirs, and your crown is greater than theirs. And Your Master can be trusted to pay you for your work.

6. To learn Torah is greater than to be a *Kohein* (*Gadol*) or a king. A king has thirty advantages, and a *Kohein* (*Gadol*) has twenty-four. But in order to gain Torah learning a person must improve himself in forty-eight ways. They are: study, listening carefully, saying the lessons aloud, understanding in the heart, awe of his teachers, fear of heaven, humbleness, joy, purity, serving the wise, being close with fellow students, discussing with students, calmness, knowledge of *Tanach*, knowledge of *Mishnah*, doing less business activity, doing less worldly activity, having less physical pleasure, less sleep, less useless chatter, less merry-making, being slow to anger, having a good heart, faith in the Sages,

[ד] כָּךְ הִיא דַרְכָּהּ שֶׁל תּוֹרָה: פַּת בַּמֶּלַח תֹּאכֵל, וּמַיִם בַּמְּשׂוּרָה תִּשְׁתֶּה, וְעַל הָאָרֶץ תִּישָׁן, וְחַיֵּי צַעַר תִּחְיֶה, וּבַתּוֹרָה אַתָּה עָמֵל; אִם אַתָּה עוֹשֶׂה כֵן, "אַשְׁרֶיךָ וְטוֹב לָךְ": "אַשְׁרֶיךָ" — בָּעוֹלָם הַזֶּה, "וְטוֹב לָךְ" — לָעוֹלָם הַבָּא.

[ה] אַל תְּבַקֵּשׁ גְּדֻלָּה לְעַצְמְךָ, וְאַל תַּחְמֹד כָּבוֹד; יוֹתֵר מִלִּמּוּדֶךָ עֲשֵׂה. וְאַל תִּתְאַוֶּה לְשֻׁלְחָנָם שֶׁל מְלָכִים, שֶׁשֻּׁלְחָנְךָ גָּדוֹל מִשֻּׁלְחָנָם, וְכִתְרְךָ גָּדוֹל מִכִּתְרָם; וְנֶאֱמָן הוּא בַּעַל מְלַאכְתְּךָ, שֶׁיְּשַׁלֶּם לְךָ שְׂכַר פְּעֻלָּתֶךָ.

[ו] גְּדוֹלָה תוֹרָה יוֹתֵר מִן הַכְּהֻנָּה וּמִן הַמַּלְכוּת, שֶׁהַמַּלְכוּת נִקְנֵית בִּשְׁלֹשִׁים מַעֲלוֹת, וְהַכְּהֻנָּה נִקְנֵית בְּעֶשְׂרִים וְאַרְבָּעָה, וְהַתּוֹרָה נִקְנֵית בְּאַרְבָּעִים וּשְׁמוֹנָה דְבָרִים, וְאֵלּוּ הֵן: בְּתַלְמוּד, בִּשְׁמִיעַת הָאֹזֶן, בַּעֲרִיכַת שְׂפָתָיִם, בְּבִינַת הַלֵּב, בְּשִׂכְלוּת הַלֵּב, בְּאֵימָה, בְּיִרְאָה, בַּעֲנָוָה, בְּשִׂמְחָה, בְּטָהֳרָה, בְּשִׁמּוּשׁ חֲכָמִים, בְּדִקְדּוּק חֲבֵרִים, בְּפִלְפּוּל הַתַּלְמִידִים, בְּיִשּׁוּב, בְּמִקְרָא, בְּמִשְׁנָה, בְּמִעוּט סְחוֹרָה, בְּמִעוּט דֶּרֶךְ אֶרֶץ, בְּמִעוּט תַּעֲנוּג, בְּמִעוּט שֵׁנָה, בְּמִעוּט שִׂיחָה, בְּמִעוּט שְׂחוֹק, בְּאֶרֶךְ אַפַּיִם, בְּלֵב טוֹב, בֶּאֱמוּנַת חֲכָמִים,

accepting suffering, knowing one's place, being happy with whatever he has, making a fence around his words, not being boastful, endearing oneself to people, loving God, loving His creatures, loving righteousness, loving justice, loving to have one's mistakes corrected, keeping far from honor, not being arrogant about one's knowledge, not enjoying making decisions in *halachah*, sharing another person's burden, judging others in a good way, setting them on the path of truth, setting them on the path of peace, teaching calmly, asking and answering, listening and adding, studying in order to teach, studying in order to do the *mitzvos*, making his teacher wiser, thinking over his lessons, and repeating a thought in the name of the person who said it first. For we have learned that whoever repeats a thought in the name of the person who said it first brings redemption to the world — as it says in the *Megillah* (*Esther* 2:22), "And Esther told it to the king in Mordechai's name" and because of that the Jews were saved.

7. Torah is great. It gives life to the people who follow it, both in this world and in the World to Come. In fact, Shlomo *Hamelech* wrote many verses about this in *Mishlei* — as it says (4:22), "For the teachings of the Torah are life for someone who finds them, and they heal his whole body." And (3:8), "It shall be healing for your belly, and marrow for your bones." And (3:18), "The Torah is a tree of life for those who hold onto it, and those who support it

בְּקַבָּלַת הַיִּסּוּרִין, הַמַּכִּיר אֶת מְקוֹמוֹ, וְהַשָּׂמֵחַ בְּחֶלְקוֹ, וְהָעוֹשֶׂה סְיָג לִדְבָרָיו, וְאֵינוֹ מַחֲזִיק טוֹבָה לְעַצְמוֹ, אָהוּב, אוֹהֵב אֶת הַמָּקוֹם, אוֹהֵב אֶת הַבְּרִיּוֹת, אוֹהֵב אֶת הַצְּדָקוֹת, אוֹהֵב אֶת הַמֵּישָׁרִים, אוֹהֵב אֶת הַתּוֹכָחוֹת, וּמִתְרַחֵק מִן הַכָּבוֹד, וְלֹא מֵגִיס לִבּוֹ בְּתַלְמוּדוֹ, וְאֵינוֹ שָׂמֵחַ בְּהוֹרָאָה, נוֹשֵׂא בְעֹל עִם חֲבֵרוֹ, וּמַכְרִיעוֹ לְכַף זְכוּת, וּמַעֲמִידוֹ עַל הָאֱמֶת, וּמַעֲמִידוֹ עַל הַשָּׁלוֹם, וּמִתְיַשֵּׁב לִבּוֹ בְּתַלְמוּדוֹ, שׁוֹאֵל וּמֵשִׁיב, שׁוֹמֵעַ וּמוֹסִיף, הַלּוֹמֵד עַל מְנָת לְלַמֵּד, וְהַלּוֹמֵד עַל מְנָת לַעֲשׂוֹת, הַמַּחְכִּים אֶת רַבּוֹ, וְהַמְכַוֵּן אֶת שְׁמוּעָתוֹ, וְהָאוֹמֵר דָּבָר בְּשֵׁם אוֹמְרוֹ. הָא לָמַדְתָּ, כָּל הָאוֹמֵר דָּבָר בְּשֵׁם אוֹמְרוֹ, מֵבִיא גְאֻלָּה לָעוֹלָם, שֶׁנֶּאֱמַר: "וַתֹּאמֶר אֶסְתֵּר לַמֶּלֶךְ בְּשֵׁם מָרְדֳּכָי."

[ז] גְּדוֹלָה תוֹרָה, שֶׁהִיא נוֹתֶנֶת חַיִּים לְעוֹשֶׂיהָ בָּעוֹלָם הַזֶּה וּבָעוֹלָם הַבָּא, שֶׁנֶּאֱמַר: "כִּי חַיִּים הֵם לְמֹצְאֵיהֶם, וּלְכָל בְּשָׂרוֹ מַרְפֵּא." וְאוֹמֵר: "רְפְאוּת תְּהִי לְשָׁרֶּךָ, וְשִׁקּוּי לְעַצְמוֹתֶיךָ." וְאוֹמֵר: "עֵץ חַיִּים הִיא לַמַּחֲזִיקִים בָּהּ וְתֹמְכֶיהָ

---

6. שֶׁהַמַּלְכוּת נִקְנֵית בִּשְׁלֹשִׁים מַעֲלוֹת וְהַכְּהֻנָּה נִקְנֵית בְּעֶשְׂרִים וְאַרְבָּעָה — **A king has thirty advantages, and a Kohein (Gadol) has twenty-four.**

The second chapter of *Sanhedrin* lists the thirty advantages of the king. Also, thirty laws that apply to the king can be found in *Devarim* (17:14-20) and *Shmuel I* (8:11-21).

The Torah (*Bamidbar* 18:8-20) lists twenty-four gifts that are given to the *Kohanim*. Additionally, the Vilna Gaon lists twenty-four advantages that the *Kohein Gadol* has over a regular *Kohein*.

7. גְּדוֹלָה תוֹרָה שֶׁהִיא נוֹתֶנֶת חַיִּים לְעוֹשֶׂיהָ בָּעוֹלָם הַזֶּה וּבָעוֹלָם הַבָּא — **Torah is great. It gives life to the people who follow it, both in this world and in the World to Come.**

We can understand how Torah gives us life in the World to Come. But how does it give us life in this world? The *Talmud* explains that Torah study is a very powerful

medicine. R' Yehoshua ben Levi taught:

If someone has a headache, he should study Torah — as it is written in *Mishlei*, "Its teachings are a graceful wreath for your head." If someone has a pain in his throat, he should study Torah — as it is written, "And jeweled strands for your neck." If someone has a stomach ache, he should study Torah — as it is written, "It shall be healing for your belly." If someone's bones ache, he should study Torah — as it is written, "And marrow for your bones." If someone has pains through his whole body, he should study Torah — as it is written, "And they heal his whole body."

R' Yehudah bar R' Chiyah taught: God is not like a human doctor. When a human doctor prescribes a medicine, it will help one part of the patient's body, yet it may be harmful to another part. But God gave the Torah, which is a medicine that gives life to the whole body — as it says, "And they heal his whole body" (*Eiruvin* 54a).

deserve praise." And (1:9), "Its teachings are a graceful wreath for your head, and jeweled strands for your neck." And (4:9), "It will give your head a graceful wreath, and place a crown of glory upon you." And (9:11), the Torah says, "Through me your days will be increased, and you will have added years of life." And (3:16), "Long days are on the Torah's right side, and on its left are riches and honor." And (3:2), "For they shall add to you long days and years of life and peace."

8. R' Shimon ben Yehudah taught in the name of R' Shimon ben Yochai:

Beauty, strength, riches, honor, the wisdom of old age, a ripe old age and children — all of these are fitting for *tzaddikim* and fitting for the world. We find this lesson in many verses of *Mishlei* — as it says (16:31), "Ripe old age is the crown of splendor, it is found on the path of the righteous." And (17:6), "Grandchildren are the crown of the wise elders, and parents are the splendor of their children." And (20:29), "Their strength is the splendor of youths, and a ripe old age is the beauty of the wise elders." And the *Navi* (*Yishayahu* 24:23) writes, "The moon will be embarrassed and the sun will be ashamed when *Hashem*, Master of Legions, will reign over Mount Zion and *Yerushalayim*; and there shall be honor for the wise elders who serve Him."

R' Shimon ben Menasya taught:

These seven *middos* that the Sages counted for the *tzaddikim* are all true about Rabbi [Yehudah *Hanassi*] and his sons.

9. R' Yose ben Kisma told a story with an important lesson:

Once I was walking on the road, when a man met me. He greeted me, "*Shalom Aleichem*," and I replied, "*Aleichem Shalom*." He asked me, "Rabbi, where do you come from?" and I answered him, "I am from a large city that has many wise men and scholars." He asked me, "Rabbi, would you be willing to live with us

מְאֻשָּׁר." וְאוֹמֵר: "כִּי לִוְיַת חֵן הֵם לְרֹאשֶׁךָ, וַעֲנָקִים לְגַרְגְּרֹתֶיךָ." וְאוֹמֵר: "תִּתֵּן לְרֹאשְׁךָ לִוְיַת חֵן, עֲטֶרֶת תִּפְאֶרֶת תְּמַגְּנֶךָ." וְאוֹמֵר: "כִּי בִי יִרְבּוּ יָמֶיךָ, וְיוֹסִיפוּ לְךָ שְׁנוֹת חַיִּים." וְאוֹמֵר: "אֹרֶךְ יָמִים בִּימִינָהּ, בִּשְׂמֹאולָהּ עֹשֶׁר וְכָבוֹד." וְאוֹמֵר: "כִּי אֹרֶךְ יָמִים וּשְׁנוֹת חַיִּים וְשָׁלוֹם יוֹסִיפוּ לָךְ."

[ח] רַבִּי שִׁמְעוֹן בֶּן יְהוּדָה מִשּׁוּם רַבִּי שִׁמְעוֹן בֶּן יוֹחָאי אוֹמֵר: הַנּוֹי, וְהַכֹּחַ, וְהָעֹשֶׁר, וְהַכָּבוֹד, וְהַחָכְמָה, וְהַזִּקְנָה, וְהַשֵּׂיבָה, וְהַבָּנִים — נָאֶה לַצַּדִּיקִים וְנָאֶה לָעוֹלָם, שֶׁנֶּאֱמַר: "עֲטֶרֶת תִּפְאֶרֶת שֵׂיבָה, בְּדֶרֶךְ צְדָקָה תִּמָּצֵא." וְאוֹמֵר: "עֲטֶרֶת זְקֵנִים בְּנֵי בָנִים, וְתִפְאֶרֶת בָּנִים אֲבוֹתָם." וְאוֹמֵר: "תִּפְאֶרֶת בַּחוּרִים כֹּחָם, וַהֲדַר זְקֵנִים שֵׂיבָה." וְאוֹמֵר: "וְחָפְרָה הַלְּבָנָה וּבוֹשָׁה הַחַמָּה, כִּי מָלַךְ יהוה צְבָאוֹת בְּהַר צִיּוֹן וּבִירוּשָׁלַיִם, וְנֶגֶד זְקֵנָיו כָּבוֹד."

רַבִּי שִׁמְעוֹן בֶּן מְנַסְיָא אוֹמֵר: אֵלּוּ שֶׁבַע מִדּוֹת, שֶׁמָּנוּ חֲכָמִים לַצַּדִּיקִים, כֻּלָּם נִתְקַיְּמוּ בְּרַבִּי וּבְבָנָיו.

[ט] אָמַר רַבִּי יוֹסֵי בֶּן קִסְמָא: פַּעַם אַחַת הָיִיתִי מְהַלֵּךְ בַּדֶּרֶךְ, וּפָגַע בִּי אָדָם אֶחָד. וְנָתַן לִי שָׁלוֹם, וְהֶחֱזַרְתִּי לוֹ שָׁלוֹם. אָמַר לִי: "רַבִּי, מֵאֵיזֶה מָקוֹם אָתָּה"? אָמַרְתִּי לוֹ: "מֵעִיר גְּדוֹלָה שֶׁל חֲכָמִים וְשֶׁל סוֹפְרִים אָנִי." אָמַר לִי: "רַבִּי, רְצוֹנְךָ שֶׁתָּדוּר עִמָּנוּ

---

8. נָאֶה לַצַּדִּיקִים וְנָאֶה לָעוֹלָם — All of these are fitting for tzaddikim and fitting for the world.

The seven *middos* listed here can be used for the benefit of the world. But some people would use them selfishly. That is why they are fitting only for *tzaddikim* who will use them to help others.

in our city? If you do, I will give you a million gold coins, jewels and pearls!'' I replied, ''Even if you would give me all the silver and gold, jewels and pearls in the world, I will not live anywhere but in a place of Torah.''

And this is the lesson David *Hamelech* teaches in *Tehillim* (119:72), ''The Torah that You spoke is better for me than thousands of gold and silver coins.'' Not only that, but at the time when a person must leave this world, none of his silver, gold, jewels or pearls will go along with him. Only his Torah learning and his good deeds will accompany him — as Shlomo *Hamelech* teaches about the Torah (*Mishlei* 6:22), ''When you walk, it will lead you; when you lie down, it will protect you; when you awake, it will tell good things about you.'' The three parts of the sentence speak of three times in a person's life: ''When you walk, it will lead you,'' means in this world; ''when you lie down, it will protect you,'' in the grave; ''when you awake, it will tell good things about you,'' in the World to Come.

בִּמְקוֹמֵנוּ? וַאֲנִי אֶתֵּן לְךָ אֶלֶף אֲלָפִים דִּינְרֵי זָהָב וַאֲבָנִים טוֹבוֹת וּמַרְגָּלִיּוֹת.'' אָמַרְתִּי לוֹ: ''אִם אַתָּה נוֹתֵן לִי כָּל כֶּסֶף וְזָהָב וַאֲבָנִים טוֹבוֹת וּמַרְגָּלִיּוֹת שֶׁבָּעוֹלָם, אֵינִי דָר אֶלָּא בִּמְקוֹם תּוֹרָה.'' וְכֵן כָּתוּב בְּסֵפֶר תְּהִלִּים עַל יְדֵי דָוִד מֶלֶךְ יִשְׂרָאֵל: ''טוֹב לִי תוֹרַת פִּיךָ מֵאַלְפֵי זָהָב וָכָסֶף.'' וְלֹא עוֹד אֶלָּא שֶׁבִּשְׁעַת פְּטִירָתוֹ שֶׁל אָדָם אֵין מְלַוִּין לוֹ לְאָדָם לֹא כֶסֶף וְלֹא זָהָב וְלֹא אֲבָנִים טוֹבוֹת וּמַרְגָּלִיּוֹת, אֶלָּא תוֹרָה וּמַעֲשִׂים טוֹבִים בִּלְבָד, שֶׁנֶּאֱמַר: ''בְּהִתְהַלֶּכְךָ תַּנְחֶה אֹתָךְ, בְּשָׁכְבְּךָ תִּשְׁמֹר עָלֶיךָ, וַהֲקִיצוֹתָ הִיא תְשִׂיחֶךָ.'' ''בְּהִתְהַלֶּכְךָ תַּנְחֶה אֹתָךְ'' — בָּעוֹלָם הַזֶּה; ''בְּשָׁכְבְּךָ תִּשְׁמֹר עָלֶיךָ'' — בַּקֶּבֶר; ''וַהֲקִיצוֹתָ הִיא תְשִׂיחֶךָ'' — לָעוֹלָם הַבָּא.

And the *Navi* teaches a similar lesson (*Chaggai* 2:8), " 'The silver is Mine, the gold is Mine,' says *Hashem*, Master of Legions.''

10. *Hashem*, the Holy One, Blessed is He, created five things in His world that He made His private possessions. These are the five: (a) Torah is one possession; (b) heaven and earth are one possession; (c) Avraham is one possession; (d) the Jewish nation is one possession; and (e) the *Beis Hamikdash* is one possession.

There are sentences in the *Tanach* that teach us that *Hashem* made these five things His private possessions: (a) Which sentence teaches us this about the Torah? It is written (*Mishlei* 8:22), "*Hashem* possessed me [the Torah] at the beginning of His way, even before He made His works of old [the Creation].'' (b) Which sentences teach us this about heaven and earth? It is written (*Yishayahu* 66:1), "This is what *Hashem* says, 'The heaven is My throne and the earth is My footstool; what house can you build for Me, and what can be the place of My rest?' '' And (*Tehillim* 104:24), "O *Hashem*, Your works are so great! You made them all with wisdom. The earth is full of Your possessions.'' (c) Which sentence teaches us this about Avraham? It is written (*Bereishis* 14:19), "He blessed him and said, 'Blessed is Avraham to *Hashem* the Most High, He considers Avraham as His possession, like the heaven and earth.' '' (d) Which sentence teaches us this about the Jewish nation? It is written (*Shemos* 15:16), "Until Your nation crosses the sea, *Hashem*, until this nation of Your possession crosses the sea." And (*Tehillim* 16:3), "The holy ones who are on the earth and those mighty in *mitzvos* — all My desire

וְאוֹמֵר: "לִי הַכֶּסֶף וְלִי הַזָּהָב, נְאָם יהוה צְבָאוֹת."

[י] חֲמִשָּׁה קִנְיָנִים קָנָה הַקָּדוֹשׁ בָּרוּךְ הוּא בָּעוֹלָמוֹ, וְאֵלּוּ הֵן: תּוֹרָה — קִנְיָן אֶחָד, שָׁמַיִם וָאָרֶץ — קִנְיָן אֶחָד, אַבְרָהָם — קִנְיָן אֶחָד, יִשְׂרָאֵל — קִנְיָן אֶחָד, בֵּית הַמִּקְדָּשׁ — קִנְיָן אֶחָד.

תּוֹרָה מִנַּיִן? דִּכְתִיב: "יהוה קָנָנִי רֵאשִׁית דַּרְכּוֹ, קֶדֶם מִפְעָלָיו מֵאָז." שָׁמַיִם וָאָרֶץ מִנַּיִן? דִּכְתִיב: "כֹּה אָמַר יהוה, הַשָּׁמַיִם כִּסְאִי, וְהָאָרֶץ הֲדֹם רַגְלָי, אֵי זֶה בַיִת אֲשֶׁר תִּבְנוּ לִי, וְאֵי זֶה מָקוֹם מְנוּחָתִי"; וְאוֹמֵר: "מָה רַבּוּ מַעֲשֶׂיךָ יהוה, כֻּלָּם בְּחָכְמָה עָשִׂיתָ, מָלְאָה הָאָרֶץ קִנְיָנֶךָ." אַבְרָהָם מִנַּיִן? דִּכְתִיב: "וַיְבָרְכֵהוּ וַיֹּאמַר, בָּרוּךְ אַבְרָם לְאֵל עֶלְיוֹן, קֹנֵה שָׁמַיִם וָאָרֶץ." יִשְׂרָאֵל מִנַּיִן? דִּכְתִיב: "עַד יַעֲבֹר עַמְּךָ יהוה, עַד יַעֲבֹר עַם זוּ קָנִיתָ"; וְאוֹמֵר: "לִקְדוֹשִׁים אֲשֶׁר בָּאָרֶץ הֵמָּה, וְאַדִּירֵי כָּל חֶפְצִי

---

10. חֲמִשָּׁה קִנְיָנִים קָנָה הַקָּדוֹשׁ בָּרוּךְ הוּא בְּעוֹלָמוֹ — **Hashem, the Holy One, Blessed is He, created five things in His world that He made His private possessions.**

God created and owns the world and everything that's in it. That is why we must say a *berachah* before eating. With a *berachah* we show that the food belongs to *Hashem*. So we ask Him for permission to eat His food, and we thank Him for letting us. But even though *Hashem* owns everything in the world, He has taken five things from the entire world and made them specially His own. We can understand this through an example.

If someone owns a house, the furniture in the house belongs to him. So do the window shades, the pots and pans, the towels, the *mezuzos*, and all things in all the rooms of the house. Still, there are certain things that are especially his — his chair at the head of the table, his bed, his robe. Really he owns all the chairs, beds and robes in the house.

But he has made this chair, this bed and this robe his special possession. They are special to him because he keeps them for his own use.

So it is with *Hashem*. He owns everything in the world. But He set aside five things that He cares about the most — they are for His Own use.

תּוֹרָה קִנְיָן אֶחָד — **Torah is one possession.**

The Torah is listed first, even before the heaven and earth. This is because long, long before *Hashem* created the world, He had already written the Torah. In fact, the *Midrash* (*Bereishis Rabbah* 1:1) teaches, "מַבִּיט בַּתּוֹרָה וּבוֹרֵא אֶת הָעוֹלָם, *He looked into the Torah, and then created the world."* Just as a builder follows a plan when he puts up a building, so did *Hashem* follow a plan when He created the world. That plan was the Torah. This is why the Torah is listed as the first of *Hashem's* special possessions.

is for them." (e) Which sentence teaches us this about the *Beis Hamikdash?* It is written (*Shemos* 15:17), "You, *Hashem*, have made the place for Yourself to live, the *Mikdash* which Your hands, *Hashem*, has prepared." And (*Tehillim* 78:54), "He brought them to His holy area, this mountain which His right hand possessed."

11. Everything that *Hashem*, the Holy One, Blessed is He, created in His world, He created only for His honor — as the *Navi* (*Yishayahu* 43:7) says, "Everything is called by My Name, and I created it for My honor; I shaped it and I made it." And the Torah (*Shemos* 15:18) says, "*Hashem* will be King for ever and ever."

בָּם." בֵּית הַמִּקְדָּשׁ מִנַּיִן? דִּכְתִיב: "מָכוֹן לְשִׁבְתְּךָ פָּעַלְתָּ יהוה, מִקְדָּשׁ אֲדֹנָי כּוֹנְנוּ יָדֶיךָ"; וְאוֹמֵר: "וַיְבִיאֵם אֶל גְּבוּל קָדְשׁוֹ, הַר זֶה קָנְתָה יְמִינוֹ."

[יא] כָּל מַה שֶּׁבָּרָא הַקָּדוֹשׁ בָּרוּךְ הוּא בְּעוֹלָמוֹ לֹא בְרָאוֹ אֶלָּא לִכְבוֹדוֹ, שֶׁנֶּאֱמַר: "כֹּל הַנִּקְרָא בִשְׁמִי וְלִכְבוֹדִי בְּרָאתִיו, יְצַרְתִּיו אַף עֲשִׂיתִיו"; וְאוֹמֵר: "יהוה יִמְלֹךְ לְעוֹלָם וָעֶד."

11. כָּל מַה שֶּׁבָּרָא — Everything that Hashem . . . created.
Even though *Hashem* took five special things as His private possessions, He also created everything else in the world for His honor. At the beginning of chapter five we learned of God's great love for everything He created, and how He created everything with loving care. All of this brings honor to Him. Yet there are times when we do not understand why *Hashem* put certain things into the world. What kind of honor does *Hashem* get from snakes and scorpions, from bullets and bombs, from poison and poverty? We don't know all the answers. But someday we will. We must remember, "*Hashem* will be King for ever and

ever." And someday He will teach us the purpose of everything He created.

There is another important lesson in this *mishnah.* "Everything that *Hashem* created in His world" includes you and me. We were created only for His honor. Therefore we must be careful to act in a way that brings honor to *Hashem.*

May *Hashem* soon bring the days when, as the *Navi* (*Yishayahu* 54:13) says, " 'וְכָל בָּנַיִךְ לִמּוּדֵי ה, *All your children will be students of Hashem,"* and (11:9) "כִּי מָלְאָה הָאָרֶץ דֵּעָה אֶת ה', *For the earth shall be filled with knowledge of Hashem.*"

R' Chanania ben Akashia taught: *Hashem,* the Holy One, Blessed is He, wished to reward the Jewish people. That is why he gave them such a large Torah and so many *mitzvos.* This is what the *Navi* (*Yishayahu* 42:21) taught, "*Hashem* desired that the Jews should be righteous *tzaddikim,* therefore he enlarged and strengthened the Torah.

רַבִּי חֲנַנְיָא בֶּן עֲקַשְׁיָא אוֹמֵר: רָצָה הַקָּדוֹשׁ בָּרוּךְ הוּא לְזַכּוֹת אֶת יִשְׂרָאֵל, לְפִיכָךְ הִרְבָּה לָהֶם תּוֹרָה וּמִצְוֹת, שֶׁנֶּאֱמַר: "ה׳ חָפֵץ לְמַעַן צִדְקוֹ, יַגְדִיל תּוֹרָה וְיַאְדִיר".

Glossary

Aharon — Aaron, the first *Kohein,* brother of Moshe *Rabbeinu*

aveirah (aveiros) — sin(s)

Avimelech — Abimelech

Avinu — "Our father," title given to Avraham, Yitzchak, and Yaakov, the three Patriarchs

Avodah Zarah — a volume of the Talmud

Avraham — Abraham

Bamidbar — the Book of Numbers

beis din — court of Torah law

Beis Hamikdash — Holy Temple that stood in *Yerushalayim*

beis midrash — study hall

berachah (berachos) — blessing(s)

Bereishis — the Book of Genesis

Bilam — Balaam

bris milah — covenant of circumcision

Chaggai — the prophet Haggai

challah (challos) — (a) special bread(s) baked in honor of *Shabbos;* (b) a portion of each batch of dough set aside for the *Kohein*

chassid — a person who does more than the *halachah* requires him to do

chas veshalom — "God forbid!"

chillul Hashem — desecration of God's Holy Name

Chumash — the Five Books of Moses

Devarim — the Book of Deuteronomy

Devorah — the prophet Deborah

Divrei Hayamim — the Book of Chronicles

Eichah — the Book of Lamentations

Eliyahu — the prophet Elijah

Eretz Yisrael — the Land of Israel

Gan Eden — Garden of Eden; Paradise

Gehinnom — Hell

Gemara — the part of the Talmud that explains and elaborates on the *Mishnah*

halachah — (a) the body of Jewish law; (b) an individual law

Hanassi — "the Prince," a title given to Rabbi Yehudah, complier of the *Mishnah*

Hashem — God

Hatzaddik — "the righteous;" a title given to certain exceptionally righteous people

Kesubos — a volume of the Talmud

Kiddush Hashem — sanctification or honoring of God's Holy Name

King David — desecration of God's Holy Name

Kohein Gadol — chief *Kohein* in the *Beis Hamikdash*

Kohein — male descendant of the priestly family of Aharon

Koheles — the Book of Ecclesiastes

korban (-os) — offering(s) in the *Beis Hamikdash*

lashon hara — evil talk, gossip, slander, etc.

Lechem Hapanim — twelve loaves baked on Friday and placed on the *Shulchan* in the *Beis Hamikdash* on *Shabbos*

Levi — Levite

Luchos — tablets of the Ten Commandments

ma'aser — tithe; specifically: **ma'aser rishon** — given to the *Levi;* **ma'aser ani** — given to the poor; and **ma'aser sheni** — eaten in *Yerushalayim*

Makkos — a volume of the Talmud

malachim — angels

mann — manna

maseches or **masechta (masechtos)** — tractate(s), or volume(s), of the Mishnah or Gemara

Megillah — (a) the Book of Esther; (b) a volume of the Talmud

Melachim — the Book of Kings

middah (middos) — character trait(s)

Midrash — collections of the Sage's teachings not included in the Talmud

minyan — ten adult Jewish men, the number needed for public prayer

Mishlei — the Book of Provers

mishnah (mishnayos) — (a) [capitalized], the collected teachings of the *Tannaim*; (b) a paragraph of the *Mishnah*

mitzvah (mitzvos) — (a) Torah commandment or Torah law; (b) in general, any good deed

Mizbe'ach — the Altar in the *Beis Hamikdash*

Moshe — Moses

Navi (Neviim) — Prophet(s)

neshamah — soul

Noach — Noah

Olam Haba — the World to Come

olam hazeh — this world

Omer — a barley meal-offering in the *Beis Hamikdash* on the second day of *Pesach*

Pesachim — a volume of the Talmud

pushka — small box, especially for *tzedakah* collections

Rabbeinu — "Our teacher," a title given to Moshe

Rashi — Rabbi Shlomo Yitzchaki (1040-1105), the main commentator on *Tanach* and Talmud

rav — rabbi

rebbi — a Torah teacher

Rosh Hashanah — (a) New Year's Day; (b) a volume of the Talmud

Rus — Ruth

Sanhedrin — (a) the Great Court of seventy-one judges which was the highest Torah authority until about two centuries after the destruction of the second *Beis Hamikdash*; (b) a volume of the Talmud

sefer — book

Shabbos(os) — Sabbath(s)

Shacharis — morning prayers

Shalom Aleichem — "Peace [or, God] be with you"

Shechinah — God's Holy Presence

Shema — the declaration (*Devarim* 6:4) of God's Oneness and Master recited along with other prayers and verses every morning and evening

shemittah — the Sabbatical year; every seventh year during which the land must be left unplanted and untended

Shemoneh Esrei — the Eighteen Blessings or *Amidah* that form the core of all regular prayer services

Shemos — the Book of Exodus

Shimshon — Samson

Shlomo Hamelech — King Solomon

Shmuel — the prophet Samuel

Shtei Halechem — two loaves of leavened wheat bread offered in the *Beis Hamikdash* on *Shavuos*

shulchan — (a) table; (b) [capitalized:] one of the Holy vessels of the *Beis Hamikdash*

Sotah — a volume of the Talmud

Ta'anis — a volume of the Talmud

Talmud — the teachings of the Sages who lived during and after the second *Beis Hamikdash* (until about four hundred fifty years after the destruction), containing the *Mishnah* and the *Gemara*

Tanach — (acronym for *Torah, Neviim, Kesuvim*) the Written Torah; Scriptures

Tanna (-im) — Sage(s) of the *Mishnah*

Tehillim — the Book of Psalms

teshuvah — repentance

tumah — spiritual impurity

tzaddik (-im) righteous person(s)

tzedakah — charity

Yaakov — Jacob

Yechezkel — the prophet Ezekiel

Yehoshua — (a) Joshua, disciple of Moses; (b) the Book of Joshua

Yerushalayim — Jerusalem

Yerushalmi — a section of the Talmud

yeshivah (yeshivos) — Torah academy (academies)

yetzer hara — inclination towards evil

Yirmiyahu — the prophet Jeremiah

Yishayahu — the prophet Isaiah

Yishmael — Ishmael, son of Avraham

Yitzchak — Isaac

Yoel — the prophet Joel

Yom (-im) Tov (-im) — Festival(s)

Yonah — the prophet Jonah

This volume is part of
THE ARTSCROLL SERIES®
an ongoing project of
translations, commentaries and expositions
on Scripture, Mishnah, Talmud, Halachah,
liturgy, history, the classic Rabbinic writings,
biographies and thought.

For a brochure of current publications
visit your local Hebrew bookseller
or contact the publisher:

Mesorah Publications, ltd

4401 Second Avenue
Brooklyn, New York 11232
(718) 921-900